The Ripped-Out Seam

Acknowledgments

Grateful acknowledgment is made to the following magazines for first publishing these poems (often in substantially different form):

American Poetry Review: "The Death of Compassion: To Robert Desnos." *The American Writer*: "Rattlesnake." *Blue Mesa Review*: "Dredging for the Face of the Earth" *Calyx*, Vol. 13, No. 1, Winter 1990-1991: "At the Edge of the Water." *Carolina Quarterly*: "The Hammer-Headed Foal," "In a Foreign Tongue," (under the title, "Is It OK to Say 'Heart' in a Poem?"). *Croton Review*: "Bailey's Collared Lizard." *Cutbank*: "Third-Degree Burns." *Indiana Review*: "Vocabulary," "Rumors of Suicide," "Approximate Desires." *Negative Capability*: "Hives," "The Toad," "In the Kidding Pen." *PSA News: Newsletter of the Poetry Society of America*: "Returning Home." *Poem*: "A Finer Justice." *South Coast Poetry Journal*: "Not the Musician." *The Taos Review*: "Peeling Carrots," "Calling the Cows," "Guatemalan Worry Dolls," "Waiting for the Bread, the Wine," "At the Gate of Heavenly Peace, Epcot: June, 1989" (under the title, "Epcot: Tiananmen Square)" "Goya: *Los Desastres de la Guerra*," "Learning To Speak German,"(under the title, "To Speak German.") *Triquarterly*: "The Dancer or the Dance." "In the Killing Pen" (under the title, "Slaughtering Goats at Eastertime") first appeared in the anthology *The Denny Poems 1985-1986.*

I would like to thank Poets & Writers for the Writers Exchange Award, and the Bogin family and the Poetry Society of America for the Bogin Memorial Award, both of which aided in the completion and publication of this manuscript. I am grateful for careful readings by my teachers, and for the careful attention of my editor, Stanley Moss. My deepest thanks to Thomas Lux, Eleanor Wilner, and Susan Stewart.

The Ripped-Out Seam

Poems by

Rebecca Seiferle

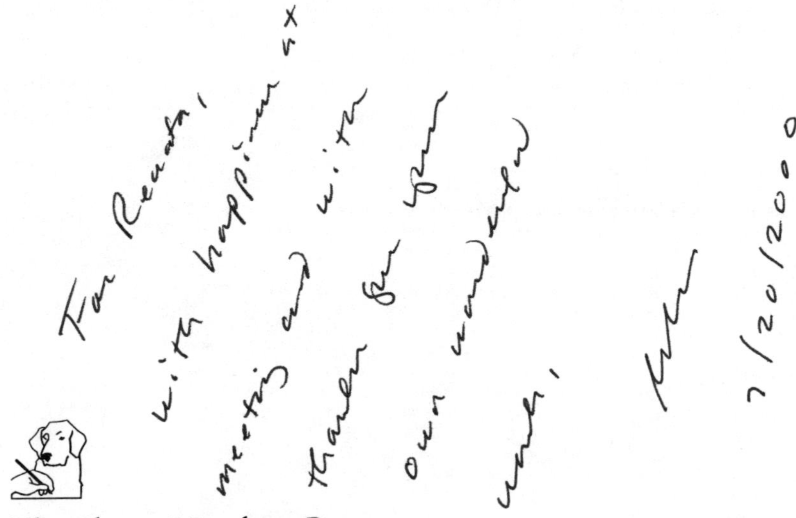

The Sheep Meadow Press
Riverdale-on-Hudson, New York

All inquiries and permission requests should be addressed to:
The Sheep Meadow Press, Post Office Box 1345,
Riverdale-on-Hudson, New York 10471.

Typeset by The Sheep Meadow Press.

Printed by Capital City Press on acid-free paper. This book meets the guidelines for permanence and durability of the Committee on Production Guidelines for Book Longevity of the Council on Library Resources.

Library of Congress Cataloging-in-Publication Data

Seiferle, Rebecca.
The ripped-out seam / by Rebecca Seiferle.
p. cm.
ISBN 1-878818-22-8 : $12.95
I. Title.
PS3569.E533R5 1993
811'.54—dc20 93-9982
CIP

Distributed by The Sheep Meadow Press.

The Sheep Meadow Press gratefully acknowledges the support of the New York State Council on the Arts whose funding assisted in the publication of this book.

For Phillip, Ann, and Maria.
To my grandmother, Nelma Lantzy Thornton.
To Grace Huffman, for her faith and friendship.
And in memory of my friends and fellow poets,
Elizabeth Stahlecker and Kitty Hamilton.

CONTENTS:

THE RIPPED-OUT SEAM

VOLTE

I.

II.

III.

IV.

V.

VI.

THE RIPPED-OUT SEAM

Nature's the same as Rome, was reflected in it.
We see images of its civic might
In the clear air, as in the sky-blue circus,
In the forum of fields, the colonnades of groves.

Nature is the same as Rome, again it seems
We needn't trouble God in vain.
We've got the viscera of the sacrifice
To tell the fortunes of war, and slaves
To keep the silence, and stones with which to build.

–Osip Mandelstam, *Tristia*

To the Angel

God allows everything but forgetfulness;
and when I survey my flocks, my family
like succulent plants around my table,
the children I rejoice to look at, I see only
your face.

Ring-streaked, speckled, spotted,
the flocks scatter over the hills
and to speak of you
while looking at them,
is to fall into the space

between one world
and another. Against you
I was bruised into being. My name
flying out of your mouth.
Each night, it was you

I struggled with, until my own body
became a ladder made of emptiness and air.
Now when my favorite child begs
for a coat colored like the prism
God hangs in the sky,

you think I don't know
it is you
he wants, your bright face
bending a sheaf of wheat before him,
your voice singing like a scythe?

The Ripped-Out Seam

I will never stitch back together
the horned toad that I halved with a shovel.
All summer, in my mind, holding itself upright,
trying to balance its torso
between its front legs, the toad has tried
to drag itself forward, to escape
the agonized coils of its own
entrails spilling out of the gaping absence
of its lower body. No
meaning I can think of, no matter how deft
of hand, can knit the pale
distended bowels, or reconnect
the webbed feet's chaotic twitching
to the brain that lunged, leapt,
propelled them forward.

I was excavating a pit for the children to play in
with their fleets of miniature cars and must have
scooped the legs from the body in one motion.
When I lifted the shovel and saw the flayed skin
resting in the blade, I thought
the thighs' cavities, bloodless
and filled with dirt, were the ancient remains
of a cat's nightly predations, or the relic
of a hibernation from which
the horned toad never awoke, but then
I saw the upper half, alive, sitting at the edge
of the heaped earth where it, too,
had been tossed.

What shocked me was how perfect
the unwounded half of the body was:
the eyes' stunned gold,
the jaw's tiny teeth, the spine's
prickled barbs, the crimson gills'

breeding color, the throat's throbbing rhythm,
the head and forelimbs trying to go on, to continue,
while the lower half had been interrupted
in the emptying out
of the blue and yellow guts,
the soft pulp of the liver and lungs.

That was June, now it's the end of August
and in my mind, I am still carrying
the still living torso behind a tree
where I hit it with a shovel,
fracture the skull,
so it will no longer suffer
what I have done to it. Again and again
the creature drags itself forward,
tries to reunite the two halves
of what it is, to heal
the wound it keeps dragging behind.

Only in the ripped-out seams
of body, of mind, do we resemble each other...
rendered together,
the horned lizard and the human figure
drawn in black on the white surface
of every vessel that the Acoma people paint
and sell to tourists. They shrug
if anyone asks what the meaning is
of this design, of that one, at the idea
that everything must mean something
other than it is.

Redeemed for a Nickel

When I was eighteen and desperate,
one roll and one can of tuna
all I had to eat in any week, I began stealing
empty coke bottles from the crates
beside the vending machines. Each
thick, green bottle, drained clean, or sticky
with syrupy residue, smudged by lipstick
or fingerprints, could be redeemed
for a nickel; I could carry a couple of dollars worth
in a laundry sack. I thought then it was a unique
misery, shuffling with a hunchback of glass
down a dormitory hall, hoping the sound
of the almost breaking
would not give me away, but, now...
now, twenty years later,
it seems only the beginning
of a common age–iron or bronze,
some new millennium, some other human age.
For every morning as I run
some errand, take my children to school,
a car or a pickup, packed with an entire family,
pulls over at the side of the road;
mothers, children, aunts, uncles,
sometimes, ancient grandparents, straggle out.
Dragging black plastic bags, like flimsy
and empty wings, behind them,
they scour the damp culverts,
the weeds at the edge of the highway
for the tossed-out wealth
of aluminum cans. Watching them,
I feel again the sack fluttering against
my own body, how I tried
to muffle against my chest and thighs
the sound of the empties
clinking, colliding.

A for Anathema

1.

In the French Quarter, a man pretended
to be a monkey so tourists would throw
first, peanuts, then money at him.
He had covered his body with strips
of that material–gunny sacks? burlap?–
with which hunters camouflage themselves.
Hue of dead straw or orangutang fur,
the fabric rippled when he leapt,
itched his armpit, spat.
When a child reached out to question
the bright blue dog collar he wore,
he scampered away, then from behind a trash can,
bared his teeth, chattered a wordless
curse. After a while, the crowd grew restless
with his trick of swallowing peanuts whole,
the insult of his rump turned toward them.
His exactitude began to chill them. No longer mimicry,
it seemed he knew, *was* monkey
even in his dreams.

2.

Tell me, what kind of world is this
where one woman can buy new sheets
and tear them to braid
into the tails of her horses
and another woman has to sleep,
unconscious on pavement, curled
against a fence? Anyone passing by
could see the pale, ungroomed,
hairs of her body, and how little
had always intervened
between her and the street.

3.

On a sidewalk in San Diego, between
the hotels and the beach, two men were dickering;
the first was taking off the many jackets
that he wore and offering them, one by one,
to the other. The other man backed away
from the foul fabrics flying in his face.
Each salvaged article had long ago
stiffened to someone else's form,
and as the first man began putting the coats
back on, he grew larger and larger.
By the time he was finished, he was twice
his size, a muffled giant climbing
the seawall, his arms laboring
against the stiffening
fabrics, the grime caked into the seams.

4.

In my motel room, I was reading a book that said
some fear being crushed
in the arms of what they are not. So against
the lips of their greatest desire, they must close
their mouths. I was trying to imagine
how they open
their wings, speechless,
as angels in cheap raincoats,

but outside the window, exiled
from the pages of the book,
the man walked away
without looking up,
as if he had already memorized
the distance he needed to travel;
his face, the sole itinerary
of that country, his agony, the only road.

5.

In Denver, in front of a church,
I rolled him over, his eyelids convulsed
as if dreaming, trying to blink out
the limitless sky. With his shirt stuck
to the pavement by vomit and sweat,
it was hard to imagine he had chosen
this sidewalk, lifted
its bottles to his mouth. He was '*like*'
nothing. His body's sour and fermented field
defined a distance into which only he
was disappearing. I could have said
he was a broken tabernacle, but the truth is
he was shivering.

Bat in a Jar

The jar was a mason jar, made to preserve
apricots and stone cherries and to withstand
the extremes of cold air and hot water baths
where the steam, rising, lifts
the canner's black lid
only to drop it, hissing, again. And the bat,
trapped inside knew, if it knew anything,
it would never escape, though
the sky kept humming
with insects and the orchards darkened
as usual, *apparently* the same.

Someone had put the bat in a jar–to avoid
bites and disease or to protect
the bat itself from house cats and dogs?
In any case, the bat kept calling
for rescue, measuring what confined it, trying
to scale the horizon, that sky of glass. But though
the bat's ears shaped themselves
to the echo, though the echo
filled the glass, the jar parodied
the bat's longing and gave back
nothing of itself.

Mirrored, only the bat was mirrored. Its fear
inaudible except to itself, confined
to its own mind. That which enabled
the bat to select a mosquito
or to nip a June beetle out of the air
now sickened it. Open-mouthed,
wings beating hopefully, hopelessly, the bat
lifted its wing like one seamless membrane
and again and again
tried to answer.

Funny Cars

At first he felt only
what was missing, woke up
screaming with an invisible
charley horse, or itched
on humid days to scratch
an absent toe. Now, he saw
his lost limb lounging in every
sunbather's flexed ankle, muscled thigh,
tanning, publicly, beside a pool.
He had gone swimming only once
before he knew how it disturbed
them, whole, un-interrupted,
when they realized he had to,
was going to, unlatch
his artificial leg and leave it, half-buried
beneath a towel. Fiberglass
couldn't take the weight
of what he had to carry.
And, immersed, swimming,
the leg would have buoyed him up,
made him drift like a warning marker
into the pool's dead end. The leg
never fit properly, a little
too long, made each level
a pitch of concrete
that he had to tilt into
all morning, throwing his weight
the other way, just to keep
from falling. At work,
when he had to rescue
a load of soaked sheets
from a failing washer and move
it to another, he could barely manage
water's eight pounds to the gallon.
So he talked about racing;

what he liked were funny cars,
those contrived, cut apart,
welded back together, machines
that lit up the local dirt track
every Saturday night, the roar
of their engines making the night human
with the sound of going somewhere,
until they spun out, threw
a rod, a gasket, blew a tire.
When he went home, unfastened his leg,
it made sense–even looking at it
from across the room, generic,
engineered to an anonymous fit–
that the body lies down in its own
dirt and gravel, becomes
a roadway and forgets us.

That's Why

We would suffer almost anything to be
remembered. That's why in the room
where the electrical current soundlessly
scorches its track along the buried
nerves, the worst terror–lying
on sweating concrete, curled up, waiting,
like a man buried beneath his own corpse–
is of being forgotten. That one was never a human being,
never a son or a daughter, but without
addresses or toasters, widowed mothers
or postal clerks, postcards arriving
each morning, was never more than
a shard of matter, colorless
except where branding irons
have pressed into the peninsulas
of one's body.

Even in frivolous circumstances, everything
diced up for the appearance it makes
on a waiter's professionally generous tray,
a woman will laugh–the chill
surging through her throat–as an acquaintance
recounts an embarrassing moment
she took trouble to forget, thinking
it is better to be remembered
than to overlooked like the ice
tossed out with the disposable cups.
Because it isn't so much an eternal weight
that weighs down on these words
or makes us speechless before one another,
as it is this sense of our own history
being confirmed by another's eyes. In you
and in you and in you and in you,
everything is worth remembering. For
some are free and others are not,

and a few, who outweigh the rest, are even now,
fearing another afternoon of electrocution,
twitching in the extremities of concrete, waiting
for the one look that could turn them back, back
into human beings.

Guatemalan Worry Dolls

$2.00 with 25% off for liquidation
buys the entire family; their tiny limbs
cropped to fit the space between them,
six of them squeeze into one
thumb-sized house, plaited of straw
like that house in fairy tales
that no one is safe in,
and which they have dyed, knowingly,
with the colors of their fear:
crimson doorways, blue-as-corpse shutters,
piss yellow steps.

One boy smiles without eyes
while a bare wire pokes through the cuff
of his pants, and some of the girls–
or are they women?–have no legs at all
beneath their skirts. Their hair,
just their native soil
glued to the top of their skulls,
rubs off easily, for what welds them together
is some paste of corn and spit.

Ordinary as the laboring days of the week,
the six of them are always searching
for the seventh, the one who disappears
while talking of miracles and peace.
For them, there is no rest; each night,
a child confesses her worries
to each one before burying them all
beneath her pillow, as if they
with their missing eyes and fingers
could bridge the swollen rivers, harvest
the life-sized fields, bake a sugared maize cake,
or, perhaps, *Madre Dios*, empty the machineguns
of the soldiers who have fallen asleep.

It must be true–these tiny figures
must travel, must scuff their shoes
on some road, for they bear the same scars
as those who made them: the red hair of pellagra,
the bellies distended with worms, the appendages
blackened by the National Guard–and, there, beneath
the imperfectly sutured halves of the body–
the fractured, splitting, seam.

Goya: *Los Desastres de la Guerra*

The fevered corpse, writing "*Nada*"
on a white slate, could be anyone,
an apocalyptic Everyman,
holding his own gravestone between his fingers,
his flesh dissolving into
the black ink, the finished figures.

Nameless,
spitting out fluid, dying,
but still struggling to kill, generic
as the women dragged off
toward a dark multitude of faces
while a baby tossed against the wall
cries in a single puddle of light.

But individual. More individual
than any hero, like Agostina de Aragon
who, finding the artillery silenced,
stood, precariously, upon the corpses
of the Spanish dead and, taking aim, lifted
a torch between two darknesses
to fire the cannon again.

Yet we recognize these people, their faces
dusted with fear and mortar. How they go on,
for years, for centuries–a white handkerchief
pressed to one's nose–searching for a loved one,
the one body, in a field of remains, or clutching
like all the world, a single shoe
found at the edge of a common grave.

The Belief in the Center of the World

They emerge dancing, arranged
in descending order: first, the ancient ones,
stiff-kneed and bent-backed, then their sons
and daughters, upright, prosperous, well-fleshed
round faces sweating from the exertion,
finally, the children mimicking
every movement that precedes
them, trying to coordinate their tiny rattles
with the controlled stumbling but never falling
shuffle of their feet: What spills
from their hands and the hands
of the people lining the street before them,
is the white pollen of the crushed corn
until the earth itself
turns white.

What they carry is San Estevan,
a severe miniature man,
the size of a two-year-old child, dressed
in a green and white striped cone-shaped
dress and a bishop's hat. Only his outstretched
palms, and his glass eyes–the peeling paint
of the whites, the slack pupils,
rolling loosely, no longer fitting
in the shrunk, centuries-old wood
of his face–suggest the depths
of his suffering, so that everyone
who enters his niche carries
a basket of oven bread, roasted corn,
beans, or fresh meat, and placing
it at his feet, begs him
to eat, to drink.

Each bobbing line of dancers is both
broken and stitched together
by the black and white striped turkey feathers,
the crimson sashes circling their waists,

the brown bands of their own thighs and arms,
the white masticated tenderness of the deer skin skirts,
the pink and orange and crimson blooms
flowering in the headdresses of the women, the
peacock feathers imported from China, the
evergreen branches plucked and carried
from Mt. Taylor, its extinct volcanic crest
overshadowing the distance
beyond the mesa's edge.

Each year the procession circles the mesa,
stops at each site of unmarked but memorized meaning:
the cisterns where the rainwater collects,
the kiva's white ladder, the door
of the oldest grandmother on the mesa,
she who stands there raising
her closed hands to her closed mouth
over and over again. Each time
the procession pauses, someone else shoulders
the saint, someone else bears
the wooden cross. While the drum
that never stops beating
reverberates down through the mesa's
layers of geologic time, a young man
rings, continually, a single hand held bell.

When it is over,
when the dog, cooling its belly
in the mud of the sacred pool, is too sated
to growl at strangers,
when the oven baked bread has all been eaten,
when the saint's niche has been filled
to overflowing and the offerings divided
among the clans, when the elders have touched
the hands of each one of their people,
the bell in the tower stops ringing,
for this day, for this year, stops
trying to call home
the twelve Acoma children
who were taken, in 1629, into slavery,
in exchange for the 'gift' of the bell.

The Draft of the Invented

In the name of the company he worked for,
its red logo of power bolts stitched
to his right shirt pocket, he inched
along the mezzanine deck, his hip clanking
with the tools fastened to his belt,
while the turbine beneath and beside him,
like the polished belly of a stationary,
measureless beast, hummed and throbbed
to its own ceaseless generation,
sending it into the breaker boxes, toward
the outstretched steel girders,
waiting for the blue arc
to connect, to light up and cool
the sweating summer night a thousand miles away
in Phoenix, Tucson, San Diego.
He was threading a wire, laying
another line of conduit
in the electrical network
that stretched from one city
to another. But nothing
in that vast invisible web
connected *him* to
the steel girders, the platform deck,
the rounded flanks of the turbine, everything
which he clutched at, missed.

At the Gate of Heavenly Peace, *Epcot*: June, 1989

—for Eleanor Wilner

When the acrobat whistling into the microphone
mimicked a quail chick running for cover
and the shriek of something descending after
in some hunger of metal or mind, I was not in China,
not the real China, but one invented, recreated,
in the fiction of Florida. And yet for a moment, Eleanor,
I could almost see, by means of his voice and his gestures,
I could almost see floating in the courtyard above us, the image
of something being rendered, a great flowering
before the applause, before being
was silenced by being.

It was not the blood of dragons spilling past
the Chinese acrobats, past
the girl balanced atop eighteen chairs,
a nondescript silk flower cleft in her teeth, past
the man echoing the cries of birds, past
the jade figurines, past the two steel balls,
miniature earths, male and female, which I rotate
in my hand in an ancient exercise
of health and well-being, trying to learn
how to balance yin and yang on the rim of one palm.
It was not the blood of dragons, but the blood
of the acrobats and the girl herself
balanced on a chair, and the man imitating
the cries of birds. And it began to seem to me
that every time there is a great opening in the world
a fist closes upon it.

Earlier, in the pavilion, I could have held in my hands
the jade body of the goddess,
Kuan Yin, and her female attendant.
The banner that fluttered in *her* hand moved

with the same spiralling gesture
that made their silk kimonos–spun from the deaths
of thousands of worms, killed
at chrysalis so each thread
would be unbroken–appear
to be flowing uninterruptedly. So different
from the headless Greek trio,
gigantic, on the other side of the room,
eroding but wired into the upright
positions of history, memory, imagination.

The carved jade
could have been water,
as flawless and flowing as the body
of the dragon on which they both rode
so naturally, that no one
in that tiny, immortal village looked up
in astonishment. They could have been dancing
their way past the men with baskets of fish, past
the elderly couple eating lotus soup, past
the boy with a basket of wood on his back.
For the third one is always the dragon,
that which doesn't exist,
has never existed, and yet whose spine
upholds the temple of heaven,
its ribs uplifting the emergent grass, mistaken
for the earth it rests upon, its face a tuning fork
for a thousand desires, hoping to sing
in this other, truer, tongue.

A metal bar floats within each of these two steel balls
that the acrobat uplifts, spinning, on the rim of his hand;
and when I clank them together awkwardly,
still that music breaks within them,
breaking at the edge of heaven or under
the cool awnings of the shop,
as if that spiralling motion, echoing

in the bell and curve of beaten metal
or retraced in the smoke
rising from every fire,
could balance everything.

When I turn these blank, polished spheres,
words seem already pitted upon them,
words, Eleanor, which we do not want
to read, pitted into the shining skin.
But what I saw this morning from a narrow window
was that the earth has one tangible body, one
living form, the imagination could take in its arms
but doesn't, so it goes on, dying, uplifting.

Learning To Speak German

Almost forty, and just learning to mutter,
like a child, the *leibling*
my grandmother crooned,
I was afraid the crime was sleeping
in the etymological root, the umlauted
vowels, the names of the days
guttural with half-remembered
gods, tossing fitfully,
all alone in the ts-set, all along,
in the sound of the *ss* like the final
wheezing of an insomniac who cannot tell
sleep from the cessation of being.

The word in my mouth
had the round fullness of a
curse; I had awakened
and found history on my lips,
like the blue and red mucous
that they say
coats the lips of the dead
who have been lying too long unburied.
Only for you–to hear you
in the original–could I open
myself to this language, say:
"*das Wort,*" "*die Welt.*"

Returning Home

Because I have been gone a long time,
I want to buy Maria a present,
and she has seen the kachina dolls gesturing
in the shop windows, among the turquoise God's eyes
and the flat-tasting cactus candy and has been drawn
over and over again to the white and black
severity of this wolf figure, his knees
flexed in the first step of a dance.
Tapping the glass, she points
with the same insistence
with which, at home, she runs
to watch a thunderstorm gather, how
a single flash of lightning floods
a canyon with countless white waves.

The Southwest is full of these wooden
representations; in the churches, each
hand-carved and brightly painted *santo* is
nailed into his niche, as if, otherwise,
he might come down dancing,
and Christ in the rigor of his cross
twists with the sweet-smelling tenacity
of the cedar limbs out of which his own form
was carved. Not stone, not granite, but figures
root-like, vegetable, green
and growing. I, too, have been drawn
to the kachinas, to the owl
opening the snow
sweep of its wings, there, in the dense thicket
of a curio shelf, its gaze like a door,
impossible to close.

But I did not expect my daughter, so young,
to admire this violent gesture of
becoming or to lift this weight,
so willingly, into her hands.

For, yes, it is the wolf she wants, shrouded
in the white skin of what
it has killed: rabbit fur masking its own
slavering jaw. Perhaps the whitewashed
limbs attract her, or the torso painted
with a black cloud where the raindrops
are still falling, or the implied
human form or action, for
when she takes it in her hands, she holds it
to her face like a mask she could inhabit,
or a figure she could follow
dancing through the smallest rooms.

How can I explain to her
that human sacrifice is always disguised like this,
as an animal or a god? For it is said
that before the kachinas were gods,
they were children drowned by the tribe,
and later to console their parents
they returned, but so changed–rattling,
mud-daubed, obscene–they could reveal everything
but their own faces. For it was never
the children themselves–silenced
first in the sacred lake,
then in the myth's retelling–that shuffled
their way out of the kiva, but others,
moved by pity, to restore what had been lost.

But it is out of happiness that Maria
wants this figure, and when it nestles
in a box beneath her arm, she takes my hand
and begins telling me a story,
how when we reach home, our house will be
full of kachinas. Everywhere
on the floors, in the beds, in the cupboards,
a hundred, no, a thousand kachinas,
dancing and singing because, yes,
we have come back.

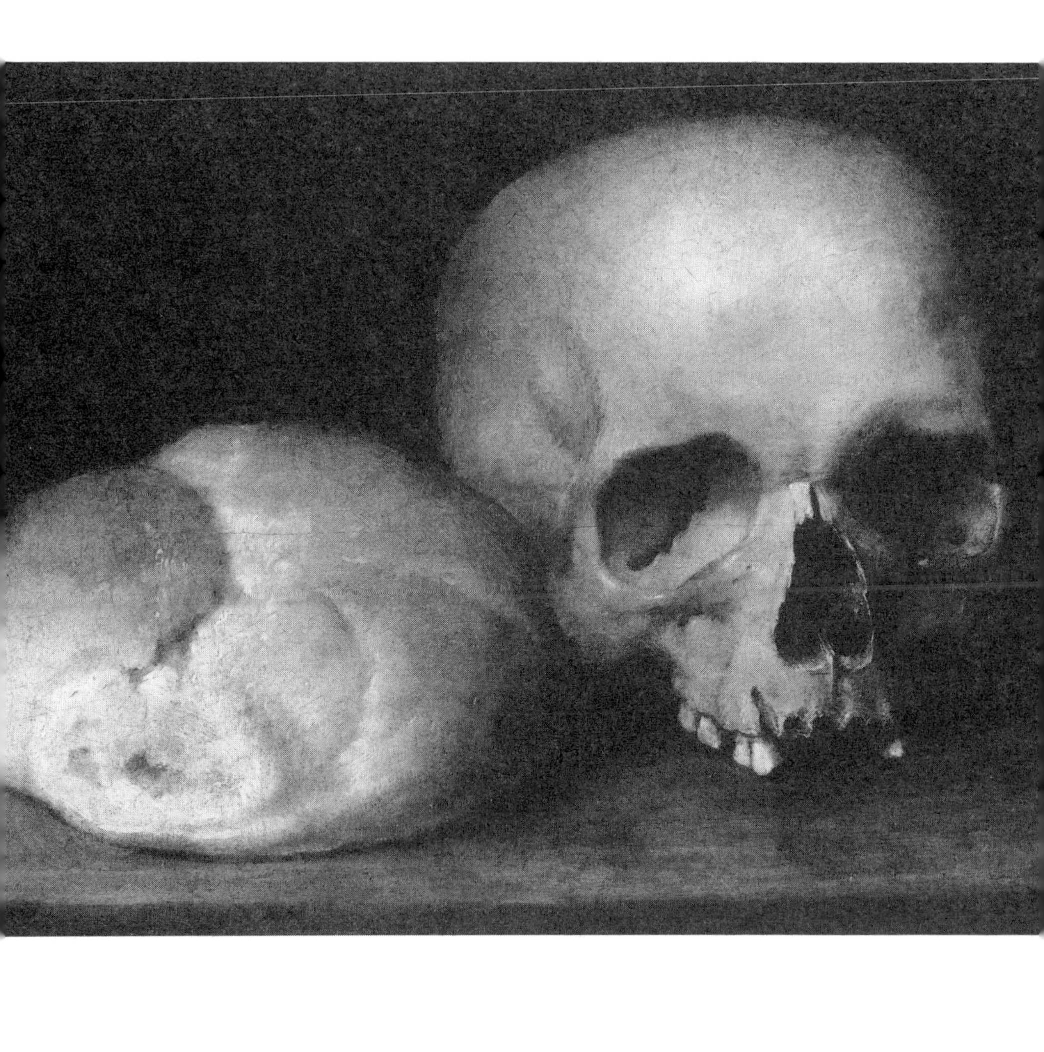

Bell's Palsy

When half your face freezes, what's funny
is the mirror, the obvious
lopsided view, or one side
of your face grins nervously,
trying to gauge if it's still all right,
while the other, motionless
deadpan, looks flatly out,
wants to move no one,
itself unmoved.
At night, the afflicted eye
never closes, but stares relentlessly
while the other, roving
dreamily beneath the lid, avoids
this vision of the body,
unconscious, moaning, helpless
in sleep. Even the involuntary fails,
stops blinking automatically, and the eye
like a gate frozen open on its hinges
admits anything. Glare and dust storms
abrade it; the cornea suffers
without its daily measure
of tears. *You* suffer
from immobility, though the truth is
it bothers others more, disconcerted
by your Cyclopean stare. Half your face
cries with them, half your face
laughs. *An evil wind, a spirit*,
the old people called it.
There's no cure but time,
and forty percent of the time,
no cure. All they can give you
is an eye patch, a pirate's visage,
a scrap of mourning cloth,

and a bottle of drops
to oil the orb. Eventually–
you remember the exact hour–your dead half
comes back to life. The left lip
begins to stammer, trying to explain
what the visitation felt like.

Not the Musician

It is, isn't it, the trumpet *adagio*,
the violin *andante*
we want,
not the musician
who with his scuffed black shoes
slaps the floor
at each tempo change
as if his foot
were a snagged fish
trying to break free.
With his white coat
wrinkled on his boyish hips,
he has none
of his melody's elegance.
He grimaces when he plays
as if the music
without origins in himself,
were something given to him,
and he had to drive it out.

St. Rose of Lima

A rose does not
always grow in the direction
the gardener prunes
it, but when you refused
to marry, how disappointed
your parents must have been,
thinking, Isabel de Flores,
a wealth of horticulture
had been wasted
on one such as you.

Only God would
secretly unfold your body,
your hands embroidering
a singular snowflake,
a winnowing of stars–all
the serene pieces of linen
you would later give
away, insisting
you could live
on nothing.

A conquistador's
daughter, how else
could you come to resemble
the dark *indias*
scuttling about the kitchen,
fixing the noon meal,
while their children's faces,
sullen and eclipsed
moons, begged the scraps
from your table?

You were made wealthy
by your face, and so painted
your cheeks with pepper, knowing
the ulcers would drive away
any mortal passion.
But after your death,
it was your body that refused
decay...that plucked rose
perfecting the air.

Not a Mere Instrument, That Voice

Later, at lunch, she wants to know
about angels, she has to sing the solo,
alto soprano, of an angel escorting the dead,
and she knows nothing of angels
except the white costume she is expected to wear.
She can sprinkle her forehead with gold dust,
but how can she voice the bodiless with her body?
What would it feel like, that feeling
in her diaphragm expressing
the angelic note?
So I try to explain
how angels are not human beings
given wings, but another kind
of being, but what can I tell her
of angels?
The hair of her neck, too actual, is
still dripping wet. She was swimming naked
when I arrived–and what I keep thinking of
is how hemmed by nothing
but a seamless towel, she entered the kitchen
and introduced herself, her voice
like a burning wing.

Waiting for the Bread, the Wine

Pinned behind this white
circular table, a black grating at your back,
you finger a fork, adjust a napkin, or placing both elbows
on the table, lean toward me, speaking
of what you have read: how suicide
can be act of integrity, if living
means partaking of death. Enchanted
with the knives and forks of this meal
that we must keep eating and drinking,
I try to stammer my "*no*" to your "*yes*,"
but I, too, have admired that one man,
his lips compressed to a pure, diamond silence, who plunges
his way into heavy traffic
and never emerges on the other side.

Unbearable, it must be unbearable
to enter the eye of God and see everywhere
the perishing, the cornea reddening
until it tears or tears, begging
yes, yes, go on breathing. We think
as long as we keep breathing
we can understand everything. But, *no*,
death's never abstract
like this conversation we keep having,
but always coming clearer, always
coming into view, like this river
that rises around us, sharpens
its waves against us, dissolves
the soles of our shoes, with its color
of the unimaginable bruise that I imagine
faintly swelling along your ankle
where climbing out of a cab, my own sole
slipped against you.

Yesterday I passed this woman
collapsed at a subway entrance;
when the crowd I was in bent to her, she said, "*No, NO,*
it's all right, I'm fine,"
in impeccable tones of politeness.
Ever since, I have felt in my own shoulders
that gesture with which she cradled
herself, believing her own hands
were another's, pillowing her head
against the crumbling curb.
For I know nothing of death or the desire to be
except this tenderness that surges
through my own body, when I see how this city's ashes
have irritated the contacts that float upon your irises
and make it possible for you to see.

From the tenth floor, the top of your head
resembled the crown
of a baby's head forced, pushed
into, crowded into this thronging, perishing,
"*You*," "*I*," "*Yes*," "*No*."
Below me, hundreds of people, each one,
a honeycomb of unmeasured
sweetness, moved in purposes
known only to them, and above and around me,
the architecture, ledged and corniced,
held out its limbs, unknowingly, to catch
the exhausted birds. I had never leaned out so far
in order not to fall as I did
watching for you, feeling
how measureless you were, are....

all the green fabric on your shoulders
which the clasp at your throat pins
together; your hair swept up
and gathered
by a single clip.

Patriarchal Forest

"el aire es patriarcal y tiene alor a tristeza"

—Pablo Neruda

10:30 a.m.: a public pool, the blue splash
teaming with children learning how to swim, to backstroke
to the safety of a wall. I am trying
to understand what I want of you, the body's lost expressions
like the sunlight scattered by
the plexiglass ceiling onto the submerged
tiles in the depths of the pool. Everywhere, I have been pierced
by this longing to re-enter another
mothering into being,
this   this   this

It was not my mother rocking me into being
opening around that inky black center, opening *because*
of that blackness where everything begins.
The scent of lilacs emanated from another
breast. Her mother   and her mother   and her mother
and her mother

Eventually I tire of reading every gesture, your palm
pressing the dress fabric, over the sternum, between your breasts–
I don't believe I still exist somewhere within
you. I went into the forest *because*
no human face was reflected
in the water, no human gesture
in the current. The river whirlpooled
around a sunken tree, then sparkled,
and kept on running.

Years later when I open a window, the room still
fills with the black sky of my childhood–the scent of crushed
pine needles, the sound of the stream

running by, outside, cold
water over cold stones.

And when a stranger, a pregnant woman, passes by
I want to ask to rest
my head on her womb, that small warm mountain
clothed in black, just to hear within it:
the insistent, shrouded word.

What Makes Us Shiver

Except for the convulsions when her eyes cracked
in spirals of light like the blue marbles I crazed,
heating them on my mother's stove
until their interiors broke,
she could have been me. We had the same
chopped black bangs, the same oval face,
the same permanently puffy lower lip
from having fallen too often as toddlers.
When they said diabetes made the fluid flow
out of her ears, made her mouth sag
while the rest of her body tightened and jerked
as if snagged on a hundred different
lines, I knew I could have been her. If
my own coma had come back, needling
insulin into my veins two or three times a day,
I could have been standing there
in the middle of class when her face
switched suddenly off.
Sometimes, the teacher noticed in time
and fed her honey, chocolate, anything sweet,
to ward off the attack. But even those treats
couldn't make us sit by her. Not because
of who she was, but because each of us knew
in our own cracked, convulsing hearts,
just how different we were, and how easily
it could become apparent, like that experiment
where a glass of water was super-chilled,
so a single blow on the outside
revealed the water's internal structure,
instantly, as ice.

The Carthage Exhibit

According to the legend hung
at the entrance, Dido,
promised as much land as fit within
the hide of a slaughtered ox, slivered
the skin into strips and so hemmed
Carthage into being; unlike Rome
whose limits kept sweeping everything into one
concentric orbit. But she, Dido,
that vague beauty on a ruined wall
who lifted her head and stared
us into being, where is she
among these ashes?

Nailed and stapled to the museum walls,
the urns of countless children
are displayed artistically. And the only woman
is the goddess, Tanit, to whom
they were sacrificed, and her body
is that of an axe or a hoe, a blade
where she is incised as if drawn
by demented children, her hair radiating
a crazed halo, her mouth gaping in stone.

In the tessarae of the temples and baths,
a lion tears out an eland's throat,
greyhounds, saliva dampening their torn chest,
clash together, and the river horse, the hippo,
drowns in the Nile of its own blood. So many
fragments, deliberately fractured,
to be cemented into one
eidetic image: an ibis impaling
a frog on its beak, a quail
in a strangling net.

Meticulously composed
out of slickly shining glass, the Medusa
has the dead gaze of the permanently powerful

swallowing their own mirrors;
five pairs of snakes encircle her head,
the number that meant insanity
so that even disorder has been congealed
within the stone order of her face.
And in the center of the room, Orpheus,
restored, ringed by creatures, is mute
and the animals, unmoving.

In this exhibit, every opening has become
a maze, a way of returning to the ruins,
not a passionate movement
going down to the sea. On this slab
of temple wall, two bacchante dance,
having just torn a kid to pieces,
and in the ease with which everything fluid
in their gestures and their gowns
clots, immobilized, in stone,
it is easy to see how Carthage became
Rome's nightmare, salting
the earth and eventually,
setting the torch to itself.

How silent we are, passing
aesthetically, these fields of ashes,
these fields of salt. Speechless
when we find in a glass display case,
the collar of a Carthaginian slave,
the words etched in its metal:
"Keep me, for I am a whore, who tried to escape."
Who tried to escape
when she went down to the water,
when she went down to the fire;
the collar still clasps what is left of her neck.
Is this Dido, her seamless veils,
her ashen, her earthen rouge?

Trying to Find Our Way Out of the Museum

Paintings from East Germany

The flesh was dissolving
under the borders of its own skin
and everywhere, disembodied eyes,
locked in, locked out,
I's of the mothers, the fathers, the sons,
the daughters, I's of the unmourned.
And what sprang from them
was a dog springing after
a rabbit; the moment, no longer frozen,
it has begun to run.

The Modern American Wing

At one end, Pan played the same witless
song, before a fountain of the earth
punctured and leaking
in a thousand places. At the other,
a marble Bohemian bear-tamer sweated
under the Episcopalian altar plundered
from a notable church. And in the middle
of everything, George Washington, chilled
on the bow of his boat, crossed the river
in the wrong direction, knowing he would never
sink on the inaccurately rendered,
un-American, chunks of ice.

And the Madonnas...

before angels
with wings borrowed from raptors,
never lowered their eyes
to look at the child that they held
like a caution and a warning in the stark
blue of their Flemish robes.

The Asian Collection

So, finally, we bow
to a colorless vase
because it holds nothing
and offers nothing
but its own relentless
shape.

A Statue of Butter

Churned out of what rises and floats,
it waits by the motionless
prayer wheel to offer
its own burning to
the burning.

The Seizures

Staring intimately into
her face–her tongue beginning to twitch
its track of saliva along her lower lip–all I saw
was myself, like a vandal entering an abandoned warehouse,
thinking I could say or do anything,
until I saw a face that could identify me,
peering back from the other side. Pinned
to the floor, first by her own convulsing,
then by the teacher's panic and our limbs
recruited to hold her down, she shut her eyes,
hoping to black us out forever.

Afterwards, she would shrug us off and cling only
to the water fountain's cold basin
to hold herself upright. On her throat,
a touch of crayon had dried and hardened, yellow
like the buttercups we mutilated,
trying to read the future
beneath each other's chins.
Look at her–the kids would laugh–look
at her. How could I not look at her? Not one
of us could look away. When her convulsed gaze
finally came into focus,
what she pitied was us.

Allegory of Love

It took weeks to steam the muscles and ligaments from the bones. The vapor filled the hallways, permeated everything, our lockers, the pages of our books. Hours later, I could still smell in your hair–*there*, at the roots, behind the curl of your ear–that smell like anything boiling, almost edible, and underneath: a hint of decay, mold, fermented plants.

In teams of two, we were supposed to skin the body, then stretch out its hide, scrape away every vestige of clinging membrane, then salt it and wait. Later, we would stuff the abdomen with cotton, sew it shut, recreate the shape of a poor rat, but lighter, strangely porous, buoyant.

I still felt guilty. After my mother described the milk barn overrun with rats, their pale, twisted proliferations, and how her father and brothers had cleaned out the barn with hoes, rakes, whatever they had at hand, I killed a rat with a bb gun. It took forever for the rat to die; it must have felt like being beaten to death with a thousand tiny blows. Like being pummelled into unconsciousness by a hard, deliberate rain.

The biology teacher had read somewhere that the best way to learn anatomy was by reassembling it. Weren't we all imitating what we had read, shaping ourselves to the form of unknown experiences? When I kissed you on the neck, I had just finished reading a book on oriental astrology that said to kiss anyone born in the year of the rat on the back of the neck.

We were awkward, not knowing how to press the needle through the walls of the abdomens without piercing our own fingers. When we were finished, the rat looked like an threadbare sock, its whiskers hanging akimbo from the sides of its nose, its eyes, corrugated cardboard, squashed in their sockets.

And the bones–it took weeks to tell the ribs apart, to remember the order of the vertebrae, no longer strung together by the spinal cord. By then you had moved away. Another sort of passion kept me there, solo, trying to reassemble the skeleton from the textbook's illustrations, to remember how it went.

Articulations

When we were fifteen, our teacher sprang a skeleton
that he nicknamed *GI Joe* out of a supply closet,
and it moved as we moved, except that his joints
were hinged together with unbreakable wire.
How we liked to make him shiver,
leaving the window open so his spine
would jangle to every breeze, or
in another smaller box, to vibrate
the actual bones of his absent ear
by whistling, humming, breathing, into it.
The lachrymal bones of the face are responsible
for everything we know of weeping and, yes,
we move because our muscles struggle
against the form of what we are.
But what did he mean to teach us
when he told us the bones had come from Calcutta
because there the poor must sell
their blood and sometimes sell their bones?

No matter how well we studied for the final
or memorized the skeletal order,
we could never piece a whole,
much less compassion, out of
so many parts. In the scraps
of the languages that we then knew–
that "*Hell*" in German means "light,"
that "*Dom*" in Sanskrit means "caste
of undertakers"–what we believed in
was inexpressible. I thought I believed in you.
But no matter how many times we tied
red bandannas around the skeleton's neck
or taped sunglasses over the empty eyes,
we could never imagine the dead
with our faces. No,
that's not true, we could easily
imagine him with a face, just not
ourselves without one.

At Home, During *Desert Storm*

Taking the corner,
her torso lurches forward
with the vehicle
that also turns, awkwardly
because of how she leans
against the steering wheel.
She's chewing gum, purple
bubble gum; at the very moment,
she takes the turn,
a violet bubble
swells out of
her mouth, and she tries
to keep from breathing,
to keep it from breaking
all over her face.

On the route he always takes, working
his limbs into a sweat, he scours
his mouth, scrubs the flat
grey pinched surface
of his lips
with the palm of his hand,
then wipes
the hand on his pants,
as if to rid
himself of the taste
of himself.

Waiting to merge into heavy traffic
she stares at me
with irritation, wanting
my car to pass. Her hair,
dead rushes, autumnal rushes,
is plastered to the sides of her skull;
her lips are slack, gaping, for nothing
is about to emerge
from them.

At the stoplight,
a man in a suit and tie
drives through
the yellow caution light;
he is completely engrossed
in his finger digging
its way up into his nose,
trying to extract
something which he can no longer
emit but which
is still embedded in him.

He stands beside
the road, hunched over
as a chicken scratches up great clouds
of dust, disembodied feathers, looking
for some small living thing to eat.
He is trying to smash an aluminum can
that he wants to save
so it can be used
over and over again,
but he keeps missing;
his foot, sliding off
the round reflective sides, slams
into the pavement.

The man wiping his fingers
and the man smashing the can
are twins. One follows
the other at a distance; both
move to the same martial
pace and the flesh
on both of their lean, shirtless, bellies,
is slack, wrinkled,
like a pouch of human skin from which
everything has been emptied.

And in the back seat, the children
were crying, their mouths smeared
with a dark stain
that had already
spread to their fingers and clothing.

The Fear of Irrational Numbers

"an irrational number has no common standard of measurement ...not expressible by an ordinary, finite, fraction..."

In 211 B.C., Archimedes was on his knees,
bent over in the dust, scribbling the computations
for an invention that might have rescued
Syracuse again. For years,
his Greek fire and apocryphal arrays of mirrors
had set the invading Roman ships on fire;
for years, the Roman had been under orders
to capture him alive. The twig
he held in his hand scratched out
a feverish solution, and he was so engrossed,
the dust smearing his mouth, staining
the hem of his robe, up to his hands
and knees in the birthing of the design
in the sand, that he did not hear
the Roman soldier ordering him
to stop. Not the second time, not
the third, and the soldier, afraid
of one who could construct so much
from nothing, or perhaps just afraid
of one so unafraid of him, of
his official sword, his martial tunic,
plunged his blade into his back
several times, until Archimedes fell over,
into, onto, his own equations, erasing
the sum of his discovery.

"...its value cannot be exactly found"

In 1801, Sophie Germaine was locked in a closet
by her parents because she would not stop
studying mathematics, but in the dark,

she still kept thinking, so her parents
took away the candles and tried to hunger
and thirst her into acquiescence, still she kept
on, expressing herself in numbers, thinking her way
toward the limited proof of Fermat's last theorem.
Released, grown-up, into a world where x, y, z,
are not divisible by an odd prime, n,
if n is an integer greater than 2
and x, y, and z are nonzero integers,
she felt like that odd prime, unique,
irreducible, published under a masculine pseudonym,
dying, naturally, before any honor
or distinction could be awarded.

"...having no common measure except unity"

In 1710, Galois, twenty-one years old,
with the face of a mischievous ferret,
stayed awake for forty-eight hours scribbling
everything he knew of group theory, because
on the morning of May 31
he would have to duel Pecheux d'Herbinville,
who had challenged him, nominally, over a woman,
but who had been hired by royalists to kill him
for his republican views. By then,
Galois' father had committed suicide,
his own career as a mathematician had ended
after six months in prison on political charges,
and all of his memoirs to the Academy had been rejected
as incomprehensible. When the candle's wick
sputtered out, he lit another. He would have to finish
by morning. He knew that a solution
beyond the already solved
cubic, quadratic, quintic functions
would require another, radically different, treatment.
And that he would die when he stopped.

"...absolute...an infinite series of fragments..."

In 415, Hypatia, the last great Greek mathematician,
was walking down the streets of Alexandria, thinking
of a hydroscope. As she imagined the series of mirrors
that would make it possible to see a great distance
beneath the surface of the water, she heard voices
gathering behind her, like rain moving toward her,
stirring the dust, striking the stones
of the houses and the street, sweeping
down the gutters, a flash flood
that cascaded toward her, closed around her.
She recognized the chorus of Nitrian monks,
Cyril's Christian followers. She tried to get out
of the way, to step inside a sheltering doorway,
but they had already circled her, accusing her,
striking her with the spit of her own name,
until she understood that they were not
water at all, but some creature
with many hands and teeth
and not a human face
among them. They plucked at her,
tore the shells from her hair, the gown
from her body, then dragged her, naked,
into their church where, flaying
the skin from her body, they fed
each limb into the fire, *scraping*, it is said,
with oyster shells,
the flesh from the still quivering bones.

The New World

As we walk through this arroyo, my daughter,
six, almost seven, years old, kicks up
the handle of a clay pot,
six or seven centuries old. Her fingers
fit the indentation of other fingers,
imprinted in the slight tear at the lip,
and she marvels at that pattern,
tiny waves scalloped
into a curvature.

Look, she says, repeating herself
and retracing the design
because of her happiness at finding it;
here, at the cusp of this hill
where long ago, it must have been used
to drink from a river
that stopped. The earth
is gravid with these black and white shards,
some inscribed with water bugs,
turtles or herons, others scored
by a haphazard geometry.

Each spring, the farmers plow up these ruins,
ruins that Henry James
said didn't exist in America,
but whose relics, nevertheless,
break the harrows of their tractors.
Because this is the first shard
she has ever found, my daughter wants
to keep looking for the whole
that the fragment fits into.

But beneath the roots of the sagebrush
where the rains have hollowed out,
we find only what we are used to finding:

the chamisa's yellow pollen,
the collected sandhills of the ants,
and, most of all, dust, the colorless ground.
Whatever it was, this vessel,
whatever it carried, is broken.
We will never unearth the whole of it,
and yet what my daughter carries home
is enough to disturb everything.

Water Strider

Here, at this pueblo, two hostile clans
are divided by a small muddy stream
that only the water striders cross freely
with the unthought of, unimagined bridges
they make of their own flesh.
What moves, tangential, across the water

has the oblique color of the forgotten.
And I was always staring at something else,
the man posing on the ruined wall, the artistry
of the handhewn door, and so I noticed
how the water striders thrived
in those waters, crossing

the bitterness of that ground.
The black and white *V*, like an organ
but sketched on the outside of their bodies,
could have been sentimental, sexual, easily mistaken
for anything else. When all along
the truth of the body

was closer to the Zuñi saying
that if you had stretched the limbs
of a water strider
in any four directions, its center, its heart
would always have been this river.
For this insect skates upon any body of water,

so lightly, it never breaks
the bond between
two atoms. What we call river is that
molecular flow. What it calls river
it moves upon, upon what holds
the waters themselves together.

Unidentified Flowers

All morning, you and I took turns driving
through the reservation, past
trading posts and Navajo towns, the smoke rising
from tin roofs and makeshift chimneys, past
two burnt down hogans, a door driven
through each wall, before the houses
were torched, so whoever had died there
would be confused, unable to return.
You pointed out the flowers, weed-thick,
blooming along the highway, their blue
like the haze of another fire. Dusting
the mesas with the cobalt electricity
of their petals, whatever they were,
of whichever family–by the time, we finished
everything, retraced our way home–they had vanished,
replaced in the cycle of desert flowers
by the orange and red flames
of another species. We looked for any sign
of their petals–the shining
five hours of their lives–having forgotten,
if we ever knew, how to identify the perennial
stems, leaves, roots. I should have known,
when I plucked several, thinking to preserve them
in my book, and they shivered
to pieces in my hands, that they were
moving past us as quickly
as we drove past them. Past
the bunched sheep, the pot-bellied dogs, the houses
burning with the fires of the living and the dead,
driving, remembering
what has been dismembered: everything
woven together, stitched together
only in us.

Buddha Seesaw

In the beginning when he
realized how many souls would be caught, forever,
feeding at the edge of the water, struggling
in the cyclical floods, he felt such grief–

She saw
they could not believe in one body
but would tear it apart
over and over again

He felt his skull breaking apart

She saw their souls
souls of crayfish, tadpoles, planaria,
caught at the edge of the water
and felt such tenderness in her body
for the blind hand discarding
what it had consumed

He saw the beautiful, unused,
therefore, undesired,
red and green peppers being plowed
and tined back into the earth,
and felt such tenderness
in his body
for their clinging stems

Such tenderness in her body
for the scar on a hand dreaming of arrows

Such tenderness in his body
for the many stalks of the cattails
rooted on land drowned in water,
snagged, burning in the evening light

Even the ordinary kitchen table was overshadowed
by a father's wrath. Even on playgrounds
children cowered. Her head labored
with the grief

He saw her running through the ruins,
becoming mother and father
to herself, like
she, who in ancient memory, lived
on nothing but the rain

She saw his mouth opening, groaning,
as his crown split
into innumerable pieces
He saw her take up the pieces
that his head had been broken into; she
began carving them into individual heads, tiny,
complete with individual expressions,
then arranged them in three tiers of three,
then, over it all, the tenth head, the final
image of the father

She heard the bleating, entire herds,
lowing of stockyards, and beyond it,
a twilight, centuries later,
when the human voice would be consumed

He saw they would wear out their sandals
over and over again to mount the bloodstained hill
She saw they would always bear the struggling
life between them
He saw the slit throat of a kid, its blood poured
out on a homemade altar
She saw the sacrifice, mistakenly, offered
in his name
He saw the sacrifice, mistakenly, offered
in her name

She held his forehead between her hands and groaned,
as the skull of both he and she split open
like a milk pod with innumerable seeds,
white fluff, dispersing through the air,
as he, as she, began growing arms,
hundreds, thousands of arms, radiating
from their single form–to restore
all the fragments, to marry
what they were
to what they were becoming,
filling all that was and will be
with that nuptial, mercy
for what is becoming,
mercy for what is

Body Politic

> Some say, *in the beginning, Kuan Yin,*
> *the goddess of mercy,*

In 1863 strolling through the grey false dawn
toward the blue union tents, Walt Whitman
neared the stained entrances and saw heaped
at the base of an ancient living tree, the limbs
that had been cut off the night's
casualties and survivors. Not
just the blackened, torn-open flesh,
but all the perfect limbs,
shoulder muscles, unblemished calves,
discarded because they extended
from either side of a ragged, dirty
wound. Because its elbow
had been shattered by a mini ball,
an arm, perfect from muscled biceps
to clenched fingers, groped
airward. Fierce work–
in the Civil War, amputation
became the preferred medical treatment,
easier to sacrifice, to sacrifice
and discard than to fight
the infection spreading
throughout the body–but Whitman
did not flinch from entering
the tent, from the muffled curses,
the dragging rasp of the saw,
or the sound of something heavy, wooden,
falling to the floor. He would assist,
help anchor the man down, and then later
pass from bedside to bedside
and try to mother and father
what was left, the orphaned limbs
of the city of friends he had once imagined–

comrades, holding hands, strolling every boulevard–
but had not imagined finding them
like this, in a hospital tent, torn
by a brotherly hatred that would leave those
who survived it, to go home, bandaged, blind,
torsos on crutches.

was the daughter of a king who had always
wanted a son, so when his third and last child
was another daughter, he hoped
she would die of exposure. Instead,
the bees fed her the nectar of the flowers,
the sun warmed her wherever she went.

Rodin had drawers full of *membra disjecta*,
the muscled calves of athletic young men,
the flexed toes of ballet dancers, arms
mirroring each other's movements,
hands locked wrestling,
the torsoes of babies, the withered
thighs of the arthritic; the limbs
created, shaped, poured by his 'assistants',
forced to specialize
in one feature of the body,
until Rodin had entire rooms full
of fragments that he would try to incorporate
in his own design. The adding
and subtracting, the joining
of extremities and forms went on
for years, but he could never finish
The Gates of Hell that he meant
as a portal for a secular building.

The king had to devise other methods:
he tried working her to death,
he tried burning down the convent,
and when she flew out of the flames,

he had her assassinated by a messenger
with a bow and arrow. But even in death,
her presence transformed
the underworld into paradise; the heaps
of agonized limbs began to flex, released,
the dead began to move
with a delight they had never known
in either world. The gods of hell, furious,
begged Buddha to take her away,
to restore the illusion of their justice.

In the lull between acts when they could
no longer discriminate
between the blood on their father's sword
and the blood on their enemy's armor,
the women and children fled the city,
took refuge in caves; their shadows,
Plato's supposed illusions cast
by a merciless glare upon a stony surface.
As they listened for the approach
of armies, looked back
toward the city and hoped
not to see the plumes of smoke rising,
they began to hear again,
the sound of the earth beating,
a chorus which they thought echoed
their own desire to go on.

So she was sent back, back to the earth
back to inhabit her own body, but confined
to an island where her mercy remained
a rumor, always out of reach.

In this painting, six leaves are buried;
upside down, their stems point airward.
One of the leaves is real, but
because of its greater intricacy,
its detail, the unequivocation

of its ungilded gold, it seems
the most invented. A horizontal line
divides the painting
into halves–earth/air? mind/body?–
and the leaves into what they were
and what they are becoming. Where
the stems become wrists, branch
into hands that turn
to face us, how human they are,
palpable in their fingertips,
life lines opening toward us,
a tiny triangle of utter blackness
at the center of each palm.

In her absence, her father became ill,
dying from what he carried
within him, his liver eaten with bile,
infection streaming from his orifices;
he sent messengers everywhere
for the secret of his healing. Kuan Yin
recognized the arrows, now sheathed,
rattling, in the quiver knotted
to the messenger's back, the bow,
slack, useless. But the messenger
did not recognize the woman
floating above the altar who told
him that only the sacrifice
of a perfect being would restore
the king's health.

Every messiah who stumbles
out of this desert brings
photographs of atrocities,
men whose healthy legs
were amputated, or faces crushed
to a weeping bruise.
Not only because the wounds testify

to incurable cruelty,
but because they incite us
to correct the situation
by inflicting the same. To visit
again the arid reaches of that interior
where Cain and Abel are still struggling,
each one, a torso without legs, without
arms, hands, eyes or ears, a kind
of sphinx that cannot be riddled
because their mouths, so many mouths,
are wounds sewn permanently shut.

The first time, to heal her father,
Kuan Yin gave the king's messengers
her right arm, her right eye, her right leg...
Because it was not enough, because only half
of her father was healed, she gave them
her left arm, her left eye, her left leg.

When I look at these images:
the shore frothing with the blood
of netted and gaffed dolphins, driven
onto the beach where they could be killed
by fishermen who view them only
as rivals, or see one
dolphin hanging from the rigging of ship
because it is easier to discard it
than to let it go, it almost seems
like killing children, children
without human limbs or voices, or perhaps
it is just that children were–at other times,
in the plague that afflicted the islands,
in the drought years, in the centuries
of famine–killed in similar ways.

As her father looking out the window,
saw the withered branches of the plum tree
begin to bud and bloom, he felt

the deadfall of his own limbs stretch, green, alive,
and wondered aloud who had saved him.
When the messenger described the young woman,
the king knew it must be his daughter. When
he arrived on the island, he found Kuan Yin,
now only a torso, speaking to him with great delight
from the center of the altar. He fell
down and wept and asked how he could
make her whole again. She said
he had only to ask for mercy,
for mercy to exist.

Even after being rescued
several times, that one humpback whale
keeps returning to the same harbor
and beaching itself. Some say
a parasitical infection or a disease
of the inner ear drives it
toward the dry land. Others say
that because sound travels more easily
through water than air, whales can hear
each other singing on the other side of the world.
So, perhaps, loneliness drives the whale toward land,
as it drives some people into the water,
listening and hearing nothing
in all the waters of the world.

Restored,
yes, she is the one,
Kuan Yin, restored,
portrayed, centuries later,
in this ink scroll. She has changed form
a thousand times, lifted and lost
a thousand arms of mercy; in this rendering,
an aged fishmonger, she carries a basket
and offers the emptiness within
to the damp equatorial streets.

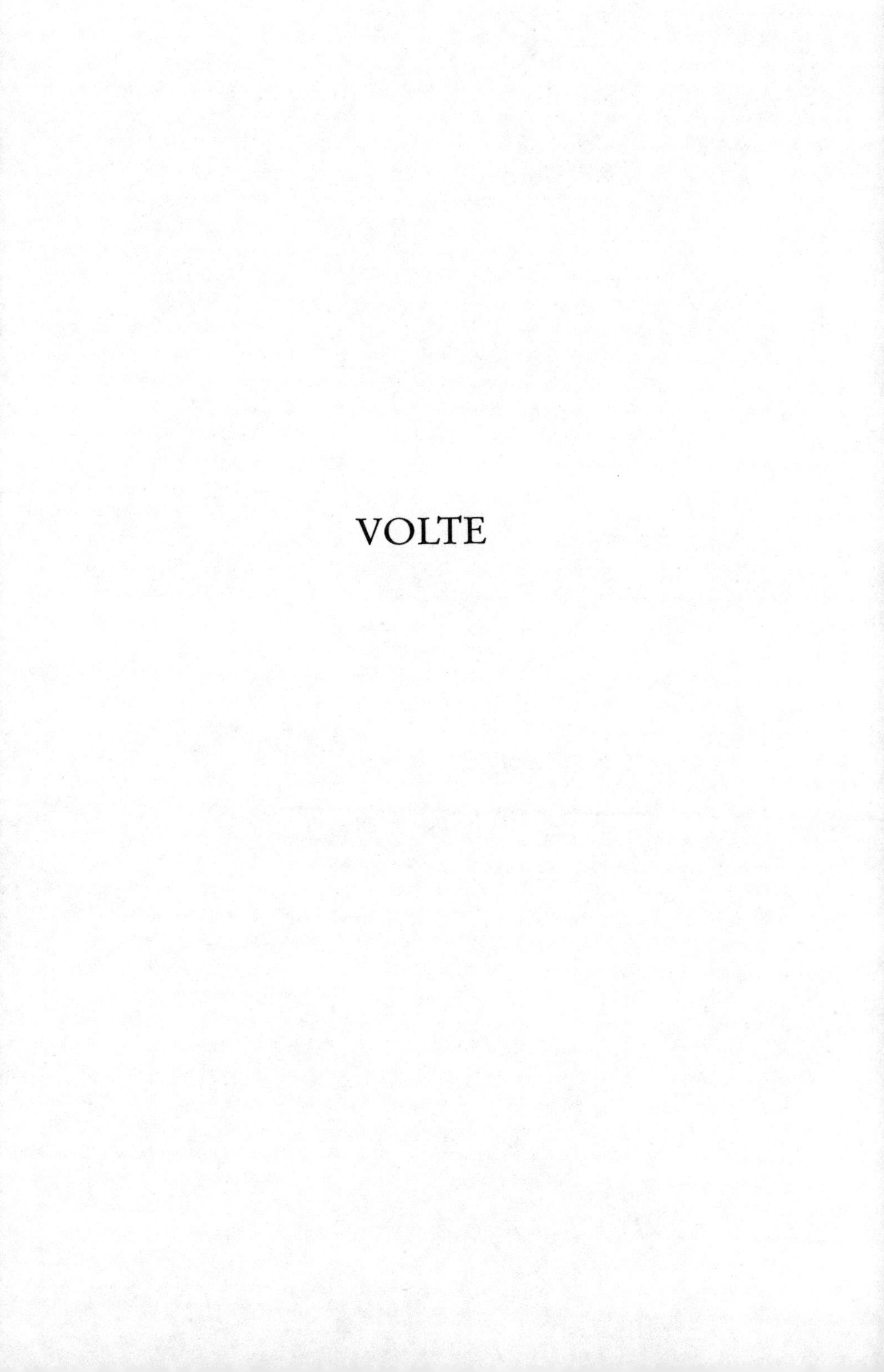

VOLTE

"...like each morning's waking, these moments of return to the world are psychic acts of turning, from passivity to action, from horror to the daily business of staying alive–as if one turned one's actual gaze from left to right, from darkness to possible light...."

"That is the moment of waking, of return; and this book, as I write, enacts the same resolution, the same kind of turn."

"...the earth in its silence, is all..."

—Terrence Des Pres, *The Survivor*

I.

Vocabulary

I am tired of the words: "bone," "blood,"
"light," "darkness." There are no angels
here. Blood is, at first, fast running
then, gradually, a clotting spray
that bursts from a young ewe's neck
the moment her throat is cut.
There is not as much of it
as you would expect, just enough
to stain the ground. One shovel
can cover it. Afterwards when
the stomach like a warm green fruit
falls heavily into your hands, you find
a few clots, more black than red,
hanging like figs
from the emptied veins. The throat
is a jagged utterance
until you cut off the head.
As you catch the folded ears
and the still open eyes
trying ridiculously to keep
the dead from getting dirty,
more blood drips down; as if
momentarily reawakened,
as if reminded of what it had lost,
another heart began
beating somewhere deep inside
where hands or knives cannot penetrate.
That is the final gesture.

As for the bones, they are hidden servants;
even as dismemberment begins,
they retain the form of their origins.
Ancestors of red rivers, they continue
to kneel to the absent grass.
The ribs arch cathedral ceilings,

ladders for the lungs' aspirations, bank vaults
for the heart. Only later when the meat
is packaged, when the dispersal begins, are
the bones revealed as the small brittle
things they are. On the kitchen counter
with muscles and tendons
like sad and stupid tongues still clinging
to them, they become, distilled in water,
a soup for dogs.

Then there are the words 'dark' and 'light'.
The goat's eyes are golden like small
self-contained suns. Even dead
hours later, they still shine.
And "dark," the empty body cavity is never
dark. But a jungle of red vines
and blue parrots, green traceries and
gentle kidneys and yellow leopard fear.
Even at the junction of death,
when the body is severed from the head,
there is no darkness, only space, an emptiness.
If the voice dies first,
the tongue thrashing in the jaw,
it is because we prefer pale meat,
because when they are dying,
we do not want to hear them scream.

Dredging for the Face of the Earth

1.

Is it the way the light falls
or the way my eye follows
the light
that most resembles
a hand stroking a face?
It is as if I were
in love with the blue shadows on the mesa–
an angel peak with one wing missing.

2.

Pedernal, for instance,
blue and looming
on the other side of Abiqui Lake,
shadowing the dead cottonwoods
rooted in water,
is masculine. Jutting, the body
of an adolescent boy.
Whereas the red and yellow cliffs
on the highway's other side
lie redundant with curves,
leading inward to the green canyon
where the water begins.

3.

As a child
evicted by my parents' voices
into the sagebrush and the levelling wind,
I thought the earth
might console me, and if not, that
then in that treeless,
tenantless space, there would be
room enough
for what lived within me
to struggle into view.

4.

How can I stand these three men
talking about the two deer
they killed and butchered this weekend?
Lining the freezer shelves,
white blocks of meat,
labelled *hamburger*, *steak*, *stewmeat*, *stewmeat*...
while outside
the tongues of the deer
freeze to the pickup bed.

5.

Does the world love us
with a love we cannot return?
Once when my husband
was feeding the pigeon–the one
we had found wounded along the road–
it began puffing out its iridescent feathers,
its grey body laced with blue and green, strutting,
then cooing. But in the distance
the face of the earth,
so self-absorbed,
never relinquished an expression.

6.

There must have been thirty or forty
scarlet bodies, black throats, white bellies,
thrashing in the basket
as the fisherman hoisted it out of the water,
then tossed them, one by one,
into the cage. But first,
he took each salmon in his hands
and squeezed the sex out of it;
the white fluid spilling out of the fish
attracting more
until the water was roiling.
Like the Hindu myth of creation
born from an ocean of milt.
But there was nothing religious
in his expression: he could have been
jacking off in the water, the way
he jerked his line backward,
the heavy weight of the treble hook
snagging another flank, gill, belly.
There, on the other end of the line,
his face as joyless and mechanical
as the fish beating its way toward him.

II.

The Death of Compassion: To Robert Desnos

Since I was a child
carrying another child
in my arms down the street
singing
it has always been the same face
I am accustomed to like.
I have found it everywhere,
in the faint music of French poetry
rising obscurely from the page,
in the shadow leaning against my elbow,
in the stream I posed before sadly
writing my first poem,
and most of all in strangers
hitchhiking, their thumbs
cocked at the sky, their hips
confident with desire.
But just now it bothers me,
the way this face
sits down beside me and touching my knee
makes it impossible to concentrate
on my own salvation.
Climbing the ladders to heaven,
how my soul turns away
when it hears the word "compassion"
as if it were a language it could not understand.
Bored, indifferent,
it jumps on a bicycle and wheels away.

You know how easy it was,
Robert Desnos,
to absolve oneself of everything,
to pretend the yellow stars belonged on another's arms,
that black market bread was all that mattered,
that to be French meant
all the inconsistencies of loyalty

that will never add, sum, multiply or divide
the small change of our theories.
You knew,
Robert Desnos,
shade among shade,
wishing the sunlight of your wife's life good-by
from Buchenwald where you died of typhus,
there was no other reason to be remembered
upon this despicable earth
than the love you felt for one face among many.
What affection you inspired among the small-time hacks
of dreams and surrealistic punsters,
who found clocks growing in the hearts of trees
until their own feelings became dead lumber,
bare planking for a stranger's house.
In this age of spiritual antics,
teach me how to put on your clown suit,
the striped one,
the one you disappeared in,
Robert Desnos,
and write this poem:
call it the death of compassion.

Stung By a Wasp

When I told you I lay in a hospital bed
and wondered how such a small thing,
black and yellow, circling the rain gutter,
climbing into its wet mouth,
could ignite my skin with a fire
nothing could put out,
you turned away from me
as years ago in high school
I turned away from the blond pudgy girl
who told me the next time a bee stung her
she would probably die.
The death that terrified her
meant nothing to me;
I had crushed bees with my fingers,
and so I forgot her until that afternoon
when my own face began to swell.
By the time the nurse arrived,
my eyes were beginning to close,
and the numbness that had begun
as a cold spot at the back of my brain–
while my husband drove our small car frantically
down dirt roads, our children
hitting their heads on the ceiling
as we ricocheted off every bump–
had circled my throat with a collar of snow,
and I knew in a moment, unable to breathe,
even the tiniest darkness had the power
to interrupt everything.

A Finer Justice

In an Arizona canyon,
a Navajo farmer hoeing the earth,
accidently chops earthworms in half.
Wondering what millimeter divides
the part that lives from the part
that dies, I am at such an altitude,
I cannot see. From the canyon rim,
I cannot recognize the green twisting
shapes, nor the man in his garden
swinging his hoe, meting out deaths
too small to measure
on the yardstick of our own.

In the Killing Pen

The bucks butt each other out of the gate.
We kill them because their sex
snaps 2x4's, leaps any fence,
smells of rotten cheese;
they are better dead than
a castrated weed-eater on a chain.
But it is hard to kill them
when they come for milk,
caprine-cute, speckle-eared, wagging
their tails like puppies. They smell
of alfalfa hay and mother worry,
of midnight crooning to a laboring doe,
of pedigree ink and mating season,
of the one we found in the snow,
of the one we carried into the house.
Their sun-colored coats, their gentle manners,
their stunning leaps, the way they cavort
in morning, shame our stuttering alleluias.
Three times a day, we fed them bottles.
Now they follow us like our own children
into the killing pen.

Bailey's Collared Lizard

It is their courage that kills them.
Surprised on rain-gutted roads,
these tiny blue dragons
still believe the world
belongs to them. No
bigger than any other
common lizard, they try to outstare
pickups, gas hauling trucks, foreign imports,
rattling down the roads
lizards take for their kingdoms.
Small emperors with wedge-shaped heads,
the males appear like apparitions
with their black collars, amartine legs,
canary feet, blue bodies beaded
with mandarin orange. Belligerent
as guerrillas, they walk on five-fingered hands
like small men doing push-ups.
The females, discreetly grey,
have the same visage, the same
imperial gaze. In breeding season,
their throats throb like tiny drums.
Dead, they hang sadly
like second tongues
from the lips of cats.
Their skin flakes off in turquoise
scales, so dry, the dew alone
keeps them alive. They carry beetles
like black treasure boxes
in their mouths; for all their pride,
they are exiled in winter. Older than anything
furred that preys upon them, they live only
a season, three months above the ground.

The Gaiety That Tore Us Open

When the black DeSoto lumbered past me,
my first boyfriend threw open the trunk
and jumped out, shouting my name,
as if he himself were a present–
all we knew of each other
was the gaiety that tore us open,
and when he fell into a harrowing machine
a stranger had to tell me:
in a country where dismemberment
was common as potato blight,
he was counted among the lucky,
he had only broken most of his bones,
but it was three months before I saw him,
begging in the office, someone afraid
of beginning all over again.

Calling the Cows

At two my daughter mimics perfectly
the moo of a cow–
"cow," "cow"–she says
and her word brings them,
jet black, brahman red, horned and milky white,
lowing in the evening hours.

What is it she sees in these massive shoulders
tearing themselves and the fence apart
when driven from the garden,
or in these eyes where the noon sun glints
a premonition of knives,
or in this terrible quietude
that under the cedar trees
lets itself be fed upon?

When she summons them–"cow," "cow,"–
they lumber out of the trees toward her
and stand there bawling
until their sides heave and shake–
as if her voice were the lost voice of a calf
trying to call them homeward
with the only word she knows.

The Toad

The toad has the patience of street people,
derelicts, winos, anyone who lives
on minuscule realities
others cannot use. Sometimes as loudly
dressed as any gangster, he does
the two-stepped shuffle in mustard-colored
shoes. But usually he camouflages
himself like death, smells foul
so dogs will not eat him. He plops along
like the soft brown hand of the earth
humming and clapping to itself. Floating
on his back, his arms outstretched,
his hands seem almost human,
but *his* fingers, tiny plungers,
find stability in whatever
they touch. He hides
in the eroded houses of the rain,
the tenements of mired rivers.
How sad he is in his wrinkled skin;
he suffers whatever touches him,
knowing his ugliness will soon drive away
anyone who does not love him.
He is all air. How large
his fear can make him, croaking
in imaginary gardens where no one hears
the ache of his poetic heart.
Where others see nothing, he sees a swarming
host; he feeds upon what feeds upon the prosperous
animals of the earth; mosquitoes, gnats
with tiny hypodermics draining away
the milk of the world. He is drawn
to the light because it feeds him.
Once in summer, I heard a knock like a hoodlum
against the window. A toad,
as big as a sumo wrestler's fist,

sat at the edge of a lightbulb's halo
and threw himself against the window
over and over again. Snaring
flies on his tongue, he hammered the glass
his bulging eyes, his myopic vision
could neither see nor believe in.
While alone the neckline of seasonal ponds,
the stringed pearls of eggs,
their clear generations hatch
and maneuver past the lairs
of sleeping turtles, until
the tadpoles fatten, thicken,
hundreds of them, big as thumbnails,
swarming out of the irrigation ditches.
Blackbirds gather on the grass to eat them;
newborn, too fresh to taste bitter,
they spill over the lawns
like surprise, like the tiny leaps
of happiness overlooked in a larger life.
They are the tiniest chorus of the river,
the progeny of the rain.

In The Kidding Pen

Tonight I am almost too late
when I go out into the moonless cold
and with a flashlight sweep the pen for signs of labor.
The white doe with the black spots dappling her sides
is already down, crying,
trying to expel a world.
Having washed my arm to the elbow,
I squeeze my hand to its smallest circumference
and go in. Her vagina tightens around my fingers,
but the next contraction drives her to her knees
and takes her breath and will away,
so my hand slides easily
up to the knuckle, past the wrist,
until I am terrified, groping:
how will I know the tiny hoof when I find it,
or tell the frail neck from a leg?
I have no vision and the goat has no words,
only my hand and her body strain together,
trying to give birth. But the insistent kid
wells up at the mouth of the cervix,
in his bright glove he taps my fingers,
and I can feel in the taut placenta
stretched like a fruit at the moment of ripeness,
his feet, one of them bent backwards,
and reaching more deeply into the doe
to straighten his leg out,
I cause her pain in my haste to help;
so quickly slipping the feet into the long tunnel out,
I begin to pull and it all becomes motion,
the goat bleating and pushing,
my hand trying to grip the wet burden,
until, at last, the head emerges;
the slight weight, the color of sunrise
spills onto the hay.

As the mother sinks into quiet and shaking muscle,
swivels her head and begins licking him clean,
my hand, used to her warmth, chills in the air,
and all that passes between us is the sound
of the newborn bleating.

Peeling Carrots

There are easier ways to peel a carrot
than this knuckled-down approach, slicing off
as much of the tender and purely orange heart
as the skin with its clinging earth and beetle scars.
There is the vegetable peeler, for instance,
with its metallic tongue that licks
the skin off everything so quickly
even a child can use it.
But just now it is the knife I want
with its clumsy handle
and dull blade sawing its way through
the closest a carrot gets to an umbilical cord,
the stub remnant of the leafy frond that once
marked the spot where it rooted.
Thick chunks litter the table; a scrub brush
would have wasted less, perfecting
this carrot for my children's hunger.
Usually I give them carrots
fresh from the cellophane bag.
But I have carved these
into bright sticks, the very essence
of orange, the very flavor of garden, because
this morning my two-year-old screamed
when we left the dog at the vet.
By the time we had driven the twenty miles
down the highway home,
she had thrown her shoes at the dashboard,
believed her carseat was the problem,
and let out of the car,
ran barefoot up the dirt road, her arms
outstretched toward the horizon
as if she could rescue or recover anything
if she ran far enough; finally
the hot ground and the stickers
wore her temper down

and she came in the house and slept for hours.
Just now she has woken up, sniffling
as if she remembers what we do not, a sorrow
that by now feels like her own
fatigue, her own body's exhaustion.
I use the knife because
this small perfection is all I have to offer.
She refuses a sandwich, a cup of milk.
Her stubborn grief will not listen to me.
All she wants is a carrot,
the bright orange tongue of the earth.

III.

The Dancer or the Dance

The wild pigs in Nicaragua,
I don't know if I will ever forget them
or how outside the ballet hall,
in front of the half-moons of the empty glasses
and the just-opened bottles of wine,
you told me of waking in a mud hut–
years ago–Somoza was falling,
and always beyond the next hill...
the occasional fire of small arms,
the mortars silencing the red-throated birds.
You could hardly remember
what you were doing there
with six or seven others,
working among the peasants,
distributing food. What good purpose
had you hoped you were serving?
Now all you could remember
was the feeling of being used.
Still suspicious of the people
who had left you in a clearing–
the jungle reaching its jagged wound
up the side of the mountain–
you were whispering among the wine goblets,
checking over my shoulder
to see if anyone overheard.

It had been a disorienting week, you said.
In the morning you were driving
the black road home, back
to your dying-of-cancer father-in-law,
not knowing what grief,
what amputation, dear God,
would greet you at the door,
and yet, in the room
where we were talking,
the wine glasses were full of light
and we were tasting

our newfound friendship for one another.
Into the goblets, down the black road,
out from the crystal reflections,
came your memory of those pigs
that rampaged, squealing, toward you.
You were sleeping on a mat
an inch above the floor
and when you woke up,
staring into their myopic eyes,
smelling them, you could not tell
the stink of their fear from your own.

I could see your ballerina's body,
those frail bones, those fine elbows–
yet strong enough to bear
your entire weight on one toe–
huddling beneath a blanket,
trying to hide from the slobbering shapes,
and I wanted to say something, rescue you,
from those pigs that smelled
of the death in your life,
snorting toward you and wrinkling
a foul omnivorous nose.

But they were just pigs.
Maybe not ordinary trotters,
not the fat sleek buckets of lard
kept in a six by three confinement pen,
fattened for slaughter all their brief lives,
but not metaphors either.
They were wild pigs, meat-eating pigs,
scooping up nests of baby birds,
eating whole rodents,
ruining gardens, but cheerfully,
without malice, like the javelinas
I saw once on the plains in Texas
crunching whole cactus,
grinding thorns between their teeth,
as if nothing would refuse to sustain them.
And it was true,

the hackles on their necks aimed
a thousand tiny spears, protecting them
from the sun, the jaguars, the venomous snakes.

And yet, gulping down everything, they were,
for all of their viciousness, only pigs.
They injured you with fear,
but, otherwise, did not touch you.
Drumming their hooves,
they wheeled back into the jungle
and left on the dirt floor of the hut,
triangular footprints,
urine stains, undigested grain,
and this shudder of revulsion
shaking along your bones.

The story made me love you.
I wanted to find the red bird
I had heard that morning
and point it out to you,
still singing,
alive. Your memory of the pigs
reminded me of everything
I ever wanted to save, the sow
I once helped load into a pickup,
how she stood in the hot sun
and fighting the rocks, the sticks
prodding her forward,
planted her feet and screamed.
Perhaps she knew where she was going.
Perhaps she had a premonition
of the hook, the boiling vat,
the meat scale, the knife.
I never forgot her expression,
not like a human being's, confined to the face,
but an expression of her entire body,
the kind of expressiveness
for which a dancer would trade her whole life
to whirl for a moment on a stage.

Hives

Erupting, wheals of urticaria,
spinning out of the body,
afflict beautiful women
afraid of becoming
the beast. So you are driven
from shade to shade,
a toad puffed
with its own poison.
Itching with a madness
you can never precisely
locate though you scratch
until you bleed. Some suspect
the fluff falling like snow
from the cottonwood trees,
but you have lived in the same house
for thirty years and every summer
it snows. Tears boil out of your eyelids.
Your mouth is first blistered
then welded shut.
A hundred red mouths
swell on your skin
and will not heal until you speak.

Volte

1.

Oh, he hit me
when I was the first to move.
Thinking he was outnumbered
or outmaneuvered, when
I was lifting my hand only to wipe
the panic from his face.
The same gesture I make now, tracing
the scar on my forehead–for years,
it has refused to disappear–but then
why did I ever believe in
such exactness of affection?

2.

It is not the body that flings off
the child clinging
to the day's narrow waist. How
it shakes itself free
and shudders! Like a wet dog
shaking and scattering everywhere the cold
innumerable drops.

3.

My mother in the bathtub
was a white petal,
a curving plant, but when
she saw me, she rose
out of the water and hid forever
the red thickets of her hair.

4.

I would like to say she leaps, airward,
embodied and intact, this woman
dancing in the interval between
two chairs and a messy kitchen table–
so much power in her body.

But like the moon rising through the vacant
branches, she twists, twists out
of her body, and I don't know if
she is coming undone or painfully,
finally, becoming.

Rattlesnake

You are the one I wanted to forget,
just green enough to be invisible,
coiled in every benevolent shadow.
Your voice–which is not a voice
but the sound of your body–resembles
the locust rasping in the chamisa
except the approach that silences them
causes you to sing.
Once as my husband and I argued
pacing our trailer floor, your voice
rose up to greet us
and resenting the earthquake
we made you feel, filled every silence
between us. Like us,
you have your narrow definitions, what
belongs to you, what does not.
We had to learn how to kill you,
uglier than most imagine
with your wedge-shaped nostrils
and the pits indented behind your eyes
to collect the death you carry there.
In Europe a poet may praise the golden snake
drinking from his well; even venomous
it seems nobler, aristocratic. But you,
democratic, without distinction
of color or geography, thrive
in sandtraps, wood lots, suburban forests.
Once laying a water line
I saw you, one of you,
you hardly exist as individuals,
tunnelling at me, your tail lashing
against the walls of the narrow trench.
You threw yourself forward,
fighting the heavy resistance of the sand.
As I shot you, you kept striking

open-mouthed, at nothing,
trying to poison the air.
And when the last tremor had forked down
your spine, you took on the form
of a river or a road, but viewed
from the other side of a distance
that has always forgotten us.

The House of My Birth

–to my grandmother

Asleep, on her stomach,
she spreads out her arms
as if floating easily
in water. But it is hard
later, to watch her
lift herself from the floor. First,
the crawling, the hoist
of the stomach, then
the tottering walk,
and all the while,
the scarred knees
of every time she fell.

*

When we grew up under my father's name,
not the black and white holsteins of *her*
milked mornings, but the black and white
highway of his, it was our own name,
anything related to us, that
we had to look for in phone books, on mailboxes.

*

While in the background, that
Christmas music promises
everything, everything
will be poured
into one cracked and tiny cup.

*

At first, she seemed the source
of all happiness with those washtubs
filled with wild ducklings
plowed up in the fields; rescued,

they swam in circles, orbiting
the iron rim. But then, one by one,
they began sinking in no
particular order. Not to mention
the others, heads half-mowed
from their bodies, that died
to begin with. So that now,

years later, when I hear a screen door slamming,
I still wake up wondering
what harvest is, this time, being
carried into the house.

Marsyas Heard the Notes of Becoming

The flute
was wounded
in-
to music
when emptiness
enter-
ed a tree.
A few holes
drilled
through a branch
let
so much
music
go,
he pour-
ed
him-
self into that doorway. *Be-*
coming, becoming, becoming. But,
no,
no, it was
n't
that music
that killed him.
Apollo
had to
skin him
so
carefully
to keep
the truth from spill-
ing out.

Almost-Human

Suppose your heart were a toad, mustard-colored, the size of a saucer, would you carry it in your shirt pocket? Stroking the ridged peak of its forehead, its almost-human fingers, would you exhibit it publicly, sunning on your hands? Or would you just tolerate it for the sake of its color?

Or would you wish to exchange its clouded and insistent vision for marbles, coins, a bulldog puppy? How could you acknowledge the loneliness of that body? For *what would you say*, explaining your angry pronouncements at dinner, your staring into the pilot light, as the reasonable acts of *any* human being?

How would you go on talking if all the while, all the while, the toad sat there, squat, mute, idolic?... and you couldn't forget the blood of the excremental insects it had fed upon...or that anonymous voice lurching out of its body?

And let's say, let's just say, you could bring yourself to publicly claim it, what if then you held it too tightly, and it pissed out of self-preservation, rivulets streaming out of its tail?

Then wouldn't you, cursing, throw it to the ground, hoping it would disappear?

Because isn't *that* the worst you can think of? That someday, someone will pull the heart from your body and you'll go home humiliated, with desolate pockets. And each night, hearing the soft talk in the garden or gathering around the light, you'll be outside, searching on your hands and knees, hoping, hoping crazily, it has managed to crawl back.

The Matachines

1.

What is a matachine?
A word that begins
with the knife of a verb
and ends with a noun's bell
ringing.

2.

The whip coils
in the space around him,
sticks out
its tongue and licks
the air.

3.

Whether he wears the face of an animal
or the face of the river
or the face of the harvested corn,
the grandfather is that one, the one
with the whip.

4.

Among the men with the faces of animals
and the animals with the faces of men,
La Malinche,
the girl child, dancing
in her white dress, white veil,

as if she were getting married
or going to eat the Body of Christ
is the only
recognizable human being,
for she has cried out
as her mother combed the snarls from her hair,
and her grandmother told her to smile politely,
told her not
to pull on her white dress or veil.

5.

What is a matachine?
That is a matachine
dancing blindly into church.

Approximate Desires

At first I tried to answer your letter about the muse: *Who is she? Is she "she" or "it" or an impersonal force? Exactly how do I experience it?* But then I started thinking about oranges. How, for a long time, I have tried to peel an orange so the skin would come off in a singular unwinding, a spiralling whole.

As for the muse, it is only when she is absent that I can imagine her body. Metaphorically, I could say she has the shape of my death. Or, that all night I search for her body's pressure points, the places where the black water pools. All the intersections...the elbow's agony, the aching memory at the back of the skull. On the other hand, sometimes she could be a book I fall asleep reading, a reluctant text I am holding in my arms. Whatever the case, her legs glide across the sheets, naming everything that is. but, in the morning, there is never anything left but clouds passing quickly over ordinary earth.

Which is to say, it is only when she is absent that I can imagine her body or even that she *has* a body. Which is to say, when she comes into this room, she is less than a leaf dancing across the unswept floor.

But no matter how carefully I hold the knife, my hands usually slip and the peel tears apart in my hands. Sometimes this happens just as I'm approaching the end of it, just as I can smell the sweet lightness of the orange, freed from the gravity of its juice, flesh, seeds, into the final perfection of its form.

On the other hand, I have often wished to fold your letter with its preoccupations into a comic airplane, an airplane with triangular wings, so I could send it flying across the orchestra pit, above the snare drums and maudlin violas, just to make her laugh. Because, let's face it, the muse has no music. She has no instrument of her own. Only her own sadness which she refuses to play.

Twenty years ago, one afternoon, when I first began writing, by sheer luck, I managed to peel an orange whole. It seemed so easy–the orange wheeling in my hands like a baseball or a gyroscope, the skin falling away effortlessly–I wanted to keep it for a souvenir. What a mistake that was! Months later, the peel had withered and become so brittle that chunks of it broke off in my hands.

Always our fathers are the ones who teach us these romantic ideals, and I can still remember mine, peeling oranges and apples and swallowing them a quarter at a time. I don't know what an orange peel means... growth, the skin a snake leaves in a ditch, the replication of memory? But it must have been true, that I kept trying to recreate that moment when the orange peeled in one unbroken spiral, a spinning miniature globe, because I thought that, then, the earth itself would begin to blossom.

But now, when the muse walks into the room, when she takes an orange in her hands and peels it, what can I say of her gestures?

Undressing the world, she finds the white belly underlying everything. And when she is done, the peeling curls on the table, like tangible smoke, like visible ash. It looks like an orange, has the shape of an orange–you can still smell the blossoms of its origins–but the peeling is empty, the orange is eaten, and she, she, it, is gone.

This is not to say, I don't still imagine her body, or, sometimes, still mistake it for my own. When she comes into the room and rests her head against my shoulder, the black words of her hair weave into my own, when she comes into the room, we branch into each other, and, for a moment, the small rivers, the grey sparrows nesting in the rafters, the oblique traffic, the restless automobiles, have this one body opening for me.

But this morning, it happened. Accidentally, that is, when I wasn't paying attention, the orange peel unwound in one piece, in one spiralling whole. But when I looked at the peeling and reassembled it to resemble an orange, its squashed features seemed comic. The result seemed empty, devoid of significance, so I threw it away. It was the effort that interested me, the juice stinging my hands, my hands unpeeling that citric body.

IV.

By the Sound of a Single Bell

> *"The iron tongue of the highest bell*
> *gave her, as it swung, its pitiful*
> *good-bye."*
>
> –Gustavo Adolfo Bećquer

I don't believe what happens to you
happens to me. In the miniature scenes

of that museum, where one is
sewing, one ironing, one nailing the floor: there is no

clay figurine for birth or dying. Nothing moves
on the streets between

the individuated houses, and I don't think
what happens to me happens to you.

Caught on a rip of metal, my finger bleeds
and curses unrepeatedly. You can't hear it,

you can't know. I don't know
if what happens to one can

happen to another. But some other metal
must pin me to you. Because lately,

unknown metallurgy,
what happens to you *does* happen to me.

I hear the loss of you humming in every engine
like a beehive waking to a country without spring.

And what happens to me must happen to you,
for I dreamt that our hands were sewn together;

the palms like faces looked into
each other, speechless at the seamless seam.

Rumors of Suicide

Everywhere there are rumors of suicide,
blackbirds diving off the sea cliffs.
Everyone understands the language
if only for one moment on a dormitory roof
when the formula reduces to zero
even the flowering dogwood tree,
the freshman girls flying at the windows,
the man with the screwdriver arguing
with his wife, the children
shivering in the parental chill.
Afterwards, survivors,
like tourists who once or twice
in their lives visit a foreign country
and return with cheap souvenirs
and dysentery, we only offer advice: if

you live,
it will be only
because you decide to live;
there is nothing worth living for.
That is what the religious call faith
and why Peter, for just a few moments,
walked on water. The powers of the city,
of the ripening fields
preserve us from nothing;
disease, pestilence, famine,
a stranger passing through, can take away
our houses, our children, our families,
even those things that we consider too intangible
to be stolen, like 'faith' or 'dignity'. So if

you expect a burning bush
to illuminate your midnight, if
you expect to find your true country
as long as you are alive, if

you expect an angelic hand to seal
your forehead with an incalculable worth, then you will
always consider yourself
worth nothing. Unique
in misery, you will not see
how all of us hoeing our fields,
shuffling through corridors of papers,
weeping over our minor infractions,
celebrating uproariously the praise
in another's eyes, are servants
of one invisible master. We live
a life we have never seen.
You will not see how. But
pruning our fruit trees,
adjusting our watches,
or driving our cars into heavy traffic,
all of us, all of us,
are walking on nothing.

The Bones of the Face

The lachrymal bones
of the human face
are the easiest to break,
so why do I expect him to
cry out, explain anything?

Even the dead
do not know what he meant to

extinguish
when he found the pistol
he had given his wife, years ago
for self-protection, and after
testing it out on the lilacs
fired into his forehead.

He must have wanted
to be among them,

the dead, their hands folded
like paper napkins, but instead, he lies
in this hospital bed, soiling himself
and sweating against
the wires that still connect
him to us.

There, where
his lids are sewn together

over the missing eyes,
the absent syllables
are refusing to weep. Though
every once in a while, he wakes up,
asking: "Did the gun go off? Did it fire?"
like us, wondering why this isn't

the end of everything.

When the Bow Appears in the Clouds

"When...the bow appears in the clouds, I will recall the covenant between you and me and all living beings..."
—Genesis

"si muero, dejad el balcón abierto"
—Federico García Lorca

Don't, don't mention the lightning or the snow falling into
the faces turned up for the view. Or
the motors droning throughout,
or the dead quail ordered,
or the water evaporating from
your glass, or the stopped
interior of
my watch. I already love you
enough, enough
to be unnerved by perishing
on almost any

scale. Though at
first,
at first opening this balcony, how beautiful
nothing seemed. The end,

the end of
everything in the two words and the three syllables of
"atomic war" spoken over
the pink flesh of a trout or the folded limbs
of a quail is still the end
of every
thing. And death

and death with a singular expression, touches all
sleeves with a gesture that was
formerly reserved for

a few. The distance between
our table and the ice-covered town,
a half-mile below, creates this spectacular view. But
in that other, unimaginable
distance, the voice itself
is falling. Now

asking for mercy in any tongue, the 'o' and the 'r'
that catch in the breath
like the choice within "history" or "horror" can be uttered
as long, so
long, as we want or have the breath
for, but not

indefinitely. On each stone that creates this fire-
place, someone has written
a black proverb and, out on the balcony,
the rocking chairs, though unoccupied,
still turn toward that
view. But because,
because I hear in any garden at least one stone saying
and saying: Do not,
do not.

Do not forget me.
You know I have nothing to give you but this
divisible disc, Hopi silver,
etched by acid into
the black figures of lightning and clouds: What

burns or burns there is the breath of this world.

Third-Degree Burns

For days, I felt the blister
growing, swelling until
my hand held only itself, fingers curled
around the globe of injury, and when
the doctor cut it open and the warm saltiness
ran down my wrist, I looked into
the peeled-back, naked face of my palm
and it seemed to wear
an anonymous expression. The yellow
lines of fat and the veins bluely
transecting the raw crimson
were a map without a country, and it took
a long time for my hand to remember
its address, to recollect its usages
of the steering wheel, the hammer, the ink pen,
to recompose its white tranquil face, and to forget
how a stranger had held it
like a bowl of milk, the skin souring
on the surface. For months afterward,
I woke to a burning inside
my arms, the nerves firing their way
back to the fingers, and the hand
at the end of my wrist
reaching for the light switch, measuring
its way back to the living
like one mistaken for dead.

Trying to Recover

I called it then
"the year of the pears"
because of the hours I spent
walking under the sequential changes
of those trees. But most of all because of
that one moment when the pruned limbs began budding,
the new growth inching exactly upward.
I say 'exact moment' but it went on
for weeks, each tree, a forest
of unlit tapers, menorah,
candelabra, what-
ever lifting
the limbs of
its own
body
in what
blessing or plea.

Cafe Without Angels

In every image of the soul
there are birds: one wounded
with a tin key, thirteen
like fingers radiating from
a single hand, two perched
on the self-same branch, one
eating the fruits thereof while
the other looks on in silence.
And that last

bird with no color, that sings
softly and travels alone. And so
it must mean something that you
are here, eating a plateful
of birds. And something, too,
that I am happy. I who have painted wings
rooted to trees, their immobility
like a wild grief

they could not swallow,
or that other landscape where
the-bird-that-is-not-
a-bird opens out of
the embryonic forms of
the dead. No, I am not sorry
to see them broken and torn. To see
them forfeit the air, become
real enough to feed us.

Verbo Divino

"Del Verbo divino
La Virgen preñada
Viene de camino:
Si le dais posada."

—San Juan de la Cruz

What angers them is the Father in their own
mouths when they step into the kitchen and
find themselves surrounded by the blue and
white plaster, the ebony, the carved wood, of
her face, the embodied she of it.

For it *is* she weighing the blue corn which
she has just finished crushing, it is she
looking into the white landscape while the
ocher pot glows beside her like a visible
uterus, and it is she to whom the infant god
and his prophet appear, pudgy and radiant,
emerging from the rocks.

It is true that in this room of artifacts,
there is one stone axe and one spear head, one
spherical and ovid, the other triangular and
shaped to a point, a time for crushing and
a time for cutting, one black against a white
background and another white against a black
background, one polished by water, the
other broken against stones,

but only the mind frames them so, side
by side, making each one articulate what it is not.
While the words themselves turn back to the
earth that uttered and wielded them both.

And what surprised me was not the priest
lifting his hands to the cup or the woman
lowering her hands to the organ or the way
both had taken on the instrumentality of their
instruments. No, and it wasn't the windows
that fractured sunlight into the crayoned
images of saints. It was the toes of that
plaster infant, those toes like any child's
foot before it is fitted with a shoe. It was
the *body* of Christ–the new paint peeling from
the nails–the body, the body, the body, the body

V.

Drifting Out of the House

You can hear them following you,
baby footsteps
so loud in the underbrush
any deer would be frightened.
Your husband's hands reaching
for your flesh–

your never wanted
to be this needed, to be
the garden
at the center of the house,
the dark core of anyone's orbit.

Look–
tugging at your elbows, your hands,
they point to the wings moving
on any branch–Do you see
the moon rising above the horizon?
Do you remember
where I left my socks?...

As if you yourself were the house
of their memory,
full of drawers, names, addresses,
where the keys are,
his shirt, her school assignment.

until after a while you lead them into
trees, pitfalls, swampy places, and
they grow angry at you
because they have to
talk loudly, repeat everything and no one
brings in the barking dog.

While the baby spills milk on the living room carpet,
you are listening to the last record on the stereo,
the last note of music drifting out of the house, drifting

into the fields where the clouds form the faces of animals:
none of them
resembling yourself.

The Hammer-Headed Foal

In a landscape like this
which could be any landscape
with its Lombardy poplars stricken by drought
and its highways occasionally washed out by rains
no one expected, so no one knew how to keep,
with its best harvest being trucked away,
and its small towns full of relatives
who find themselves in your obligation
then needle you with the debt,
you find beauty in a stranger's pasture
where a knock-kneed, bent-hocked, hammer-headed foal
totters with steps as tentative and uncertain
as those large gestures you swallow and keep
so no one will ridicule you with them. The foal
nibbling in order to recognize as much as to consume
the sheer plenitude of the fields,
inhales the timothy air,
and falls in the jumble of her own limbs.
Your own motivations are as clumsy,
but for a moment you find it possible
to forgive yourself everything,
the grey stubble of this overgrazed land,
the small monotonies of your mornings,
as beauty, still as absurd and as triumphant
as anything that ever walked from the sea,
neighs at you,
with appaloosa skin, the fleck of roses,
bucking in the sun.

The Inedible Seeds

1.

She was working at the phone company when she saw him,
walking down the street, and, yes,
he was eating an apple. With each bite she could see
the incisive beauty of his teeth.

2.

But from the beginning he was lying,
from the beginning so was she, and each blamed
the other for the women every night
between them and that one dead child
without a face or a name and
it went on for years, the recrimination that:

3.

one walked down a street
eating an apple
and the entire city was changed.

4.

He learned to hiss syllables into her ear
so that she would run toward
the door until that one night when
she cracked her head on the doorjamb
and fell to the floor, writhing,
having become
what he said.

5.

And why should I believe in my particular
happiness, in this small space
where the children play with miniature people
around the mountains of our feet?
Why should I believe I will always find
in the black curls of your hair
those tiny red strawberries, birthmarks
of pure color? And if one of those marks

has migrated to my breast
like a promise to cross all borders, then
why should I think it more
than genetic? For if the darkness outside
makes us cling together,
it is because of the darkness

that we want to go on, to populate
this room. *Because*
of that window, I still hear
that fist slamming against the door.

6.

Eventually, the child, organizing
the tiny war parties of cowboys and Indians, feels
the same flare within, that longing
to ignite the plastic and watch
the faces melt.

Good-Bye, Good-Bye

Good-bye, I have been practicing my whole life
to say to you
and now you stand in an empty street
and hold up your hand
like a broken flyswatter. You yourself,
good-bye,
are always saying *good-bye*, *good-bye*,
to the automobiles
with their windshield wipers
removing the tiny smashed insects
for the clarity of the impersonal view,
always approaching, always retreating,
and now, we look at each other, never having
found in each other,
a sincere *hello*, *hello*. No matter then,
if after all this,
I fly through the window
or am crushed under a car, my own
or someone else's: there will be no
white church, no communal singing,
only another good-bye
which all my life I have been rehearsing–
travelling, incessantly knocking
on this side of that door.

Elegy for a Gosling

Such a racket it made
in its cardboard box, waking me,
making me curse
that high-pitched solo,
cheeping, *cheeping*. Oh,
I knew it was lonely, confined
to such a small
circumference and, therefore,
mistaking every movement for
a movement
toward it.

So much noise of mind, wings
thudding against
the box, all the desire, as if
somewhere within us, a solitary
wing, torn loose, tries,
tries to
launch itself
airward.

But, always, this feeling:
shoulders turning, tearing
loose, while
the shovel picks up and throws
its few
handfuls of dirt. Sad syllable
from a repetitive mouth, it
was always *you* that
made the voices of the geese
returning in spring
mistaken, so easily mistaken.

In a Foreign Tongue

When I say "heart"
I mean the literal place,
the organ between the lungs,
the stepchild of the sternum,
the acrobat of the vaulting ribcage,
the drummer that drives the whole body,
reverberating in the blue chorus of the wrist
or along the collarbone. I mean
the largest muscle, that red athlete racing the sun,
I mean the physical fruit of the aortal tree,
the junction of body and soul
where blood and air marry in a nuptial chamber
and molecules are exchanged like money
in the marketplace of the skin.
I mean the dead switchyard, sometimes resurrected
by thundering fists, blue bolts of current.
I mean highways where inner becomes outer,
where the world lights up
all the small campfires of the cell,
and the body's exhaustion feeds forests.
I mean a city where we inhale the public
and exhale ourselves
and born, begin breathing. I mean
the life that is hidden
to the one who lives in, the foreign language
only tropical peoples speak freely.
I saw you standing in the snow.
My heart was a field.
I sat within it.

I Call You Your True Name

In sign language for the deaf, the word
"beautiful" ends
at the mouth, having already included
everything that is.

Everything that is
seamless, without gestures, the wall,
the screen door. For who would believe
this great love
that I bear for you like
an apricot tree of infinite blossoms?

An apricot tree of infinite blossoms, oh, the shape
your mind takes in my mind is
more parenthetical than my hand
feeling this table, this chair.

Feeling this table, this chair, sometimes
I wake up under a white
sky breaking itself against
the perimeters of this house.
But other times I wake up hoping
that we alone will be
poured into a single cup.

Poured into a single cup
where any look
of your eyes is like that body of water
in which I once went swimming and did not wish to
come back.

Come back. Come back.
When I feel in you an infinite beauty
inscribing a finite space. Then
how easily, how easily, the body
is borne.

Birdcage With Artificial Flowers

No, you're not here, you're not leaning
against the wall of this small invented room, you're not
here at all, oh you. Desire,

desire is, is what we're
made of, the basis of
all. But if

desire is what I feel standing in this small room, remembering
you, it's not
you but the shape I've given you. Even in memory,

it's not you among the small group of friends,
smiling down
at the floor when I walked into the room, but my own

desire to,
to take
the shape of your absence into my arms. Oh you,

sometimes I have,
driving my car across a small bridge, realized
you are,

in another but specific location, speaking your own word leaning
against the wall of your own house, frowning over
a cup of coffee which

you yourself have made,
making your own efforts to remember,
perhaps me, leaning against that wall. No,

the sky has nothing to do with this emptiness. Though
this emptiness of mind isn't without
a, a certain

clarity,
devoid of myth
as you are: actual, utterly unknown.

Almacita Creek

The only way to see cutthroat trout
swimming in Almacita Creek,
where the water is still
pure enough to drink,
is to look for the absence of color.
The blond uniformity of their backs
outlines them against the speckled rocks;
that, and the darting tongues
of their motion, reveal
their presence in water so clear
it seems it could hold nothing.

Twelve Theorems of Desire

1: that
desire cannot be satisfied unless
it is no longer
itself.

When the glass blower
pulls the molten glass
from the fire, it
could be anything, welling
up at the end
of his long hollow pipe.
But as he begins
blowing, it becomes
a cluster of grapes, an animal's
head or a vase,
and by the time he is
finished, by the time he
plunges the glass into cold water,
what he pulls forth, is
the permanent
shape of his desire.

2: that desire can
see itself clearly
only when
unmoving.

Twenty years ago,
the only light in the room
was the light
in your body
and the light
in the glass
which you held out to me.

3: that desire can always
be satisfied by
its own light
filling
its own body.

The glass-blower
rocking back and forth on his heels,
swinging
the pipe in pendulum arcs,
as if he were playing a music
which only his body could hear.

4: how desire
shatters.

The ground outside
the glass-blower's shop is
prismatic
with mistakes.

5: desire
is
desire is.

Either
the glass is round
because it fits your hand,
or the rim is curved
because it follows your lip,
or the edge is smooth
because it touches your skin, or
the glass is round
because of the earth,
or the rim is curved
because of gravity,
or the edge is smooth
because of friction, or
in any case: what is,
what is.

6: that the desire
to be
swallows
all others.

The most honored
guest drinks from
the bowl
where
the other guests
have washed.

7: that desire
embodies
its emptiness.

The glass,
in which the tiny red willow
tries, tentatively,
to root
is still fluid,
still moving, but
so slowly that no one
can see it.

8: that
desire never
sees
its own reflection.

Was I talking to you or to
the snow
outside my window? When
I said desire
should not be problematic,
I meant, that is, I meant
my desire for you.

9: desire
never steps into the river

10: because
it *is*
the river.

When I began to reflect on you,
when I began to notice the black
wires of your eyebrows, the
white temples of your forehead,
when I began to reflect on you,
you became a reflection, a face
lost in its own hair, reflected
in a hallway window or in the snow
deep on the mountains
or in the windshield of a car rushing past,
I began to reflect on you,
as I am reflecting now–
out of the sheer pleasure of describing
the white herons of your fingers. For
the act of description *is*
the act of reflection,
and I began to reflect on you
and to reflect on you was to reflect on myself,
awkward, hesitant, self-conscious. When
I felt how I felt feeling you, I was
no longer there. You were no longer
there. No longer
one laughter from two mouths,
two tears from one eye, but
splintered reflections,
one on top of another,
reproducing each other endlessly.

11: that
desire is
full of nothing, not even
itself.

The Pima woman sitting in the snow
turns away
from the empty mouth
of the pot
resting on her knee.
It angers her
when she thinks
she has put her life into
the shaping of it.

12: desire
injures the body with
infinitude.

Blue
agatized waves
draw infinite lines
in the finite
space
of each glass, drawing
microscopic
oceans, turbulent
leaves, and that
which appears
to be
unmoving.

VI.

At the Edge of the Water

I remember, at fourteen painting over and over again
an unborn child on a canvas, and the image
was planetary, a question mark
curled in the blue wash of the ocean, not a child,
but a blueprint, a helical unwinding stair.

It was 1965, the same year
experts divided the earth with warheads,
halved, quartered, sixteenthed,
while on television, astronauts
bumped into each other
in their fat white suits.

No one seemed surprised by space, the black
altitude, the cold
beyond temperature, the airless air
where everything had to be tied down.
We all knew what lived within us.

It was the earth that astonished,
that blue and green apple
poised brightly on the branches of heaven,
as if it would never
fall, yet always falling
through the fields of nothing, like a child
at the moment of becoming.

***

Wrapped in an overcoat, I slept
as if dead, abandoned
in the soft grass along a ditch in Kansas.
Along the shoulder in Wyoming,
I stumbled in the roar of diesel engines,
the stars measuring the night before me.

Packing to go, I felt the sadness of things,
the shirts without buttons, the hooks without
eyes, the abandoned comforters, our eyeless dolls.
But at the moment of departure
as the U-haul trailer flashed orange good-byes
through neighborhoods where I never lived
past hello, the view would be bathed
in uncertain light, and I never knew if
my father's Eden was undiscovered or overlooked.
Even the marigolds abandoned on the porch,
their colors intensified by summer heat, whispered
of a home unknown and, always, elsewhere.

***

In the darkroom my hands rescue
a hundred faces from the black baths
of memory. You whom I will never see again–
so many of you, irreplaceable faces!–
emerge on the photographic paper, your faces
wrenched from the emulsion
by a chemical process
I still do not understand.

***

In the art galleries I wanted to remember
the pure colors, Raphael's red angel,
the blue of Giotto, the moral lesson
of the half-eaten fish. But it is
the human wreckage I remember; how
in a painting by Poussin,
the disembowelment of a man becomes
more horrible still *because* of
the serene sky, the luminous pigments.

***

This morning a turkey vulture came soaring
over the animal pens, shrieked once,
then banked eastward, drifting down the valley,
followed by another, then a third,
all of them searching for the red afterbirth of labor
and the stillborn calf.

For a long time the mother guards the prone body,
paws it, urges it to get up,
licks its coat with her tongue.
But eventually the herd moves on
and drawn by their voices,
she cannot help but follow.

At twilight, her udder swollen, she lurches
stumbling toward every newborn answer.
And it is easy to hate the vultures;
waddling slowly through the grass
they perch on the branch of the pelvis
and take first the eyes.

But as a child, I never discriminated
between eagles, hawks, vultures,
because of any assumption of nobility
or lack of it, I was glad
to see anything soaring
through the sky's blue emptiness.

***

Stopping by the hospital to see my newborn nephew,
his face bruised from birthing, made me think
of my own child, now grown
beyond me, out of my arms
and walking away, made me think
of the darkness she had been born out of, pressed
by such a furor of muscle.

How it surprised me
when her feet kicked free of me,
even though I had known
she was supposed to emerge violently–
her fat white body like a perfect planet
floating off in the arms of the nurse.
Watching my nephew, unable
to keep his eye open
under the incubator lights, made me
want to mourn him, my daughter, the child I had been...
to think of the dark we were walking toward.

***

It is true there is no country but this one,
no unnoticed angel beside us,
and that we live our lives
for months without ears, without eyes,
without mouths for speaking,
like a welder who goes blind, entranced
by his own blue fire.

But in the particulars of this forest,
the shafts of sunlight,
the vertical trees, the vines
become blurred, welded
into one green word. One word,
if we could become human
by speaking one word...

***

As I walked the long stretch of road,
I thought of the stamps someone had sent me:
a hump-backed whale leaping for krill
off the Alaskan coast, a fur seal and her pup,
a porpoise smiling enigmatically, circling
an aquamarine pool, but particularly,
the new sea turtle, awash
in the sand which had just hatched him.

The last wave that had swept over him
still made him shine, but the earth
had pieced together
the mosaic of his shell,
the ebony collar, the grey drag of his tail,
and he was trying to paddle away
with flippers the length of his body.
Steering seaward, his lumpy head
had the benign countenance of all turtles,
a newborn grandfather's face.

As I walked the long stretch of road,
foxtails hooking into my socks and tennis shoes,
my arms lifting the five-pound weights,
I thought–breathless, my pulse reaching
its maximum rhythm–of the baby turtle trying
to attain the grace of his native element,
his back flippers, awkward, akimbo,
oaring only air, pulling him insistently forward–
and a stillness came over the cedar trees,
the junipers, the blue, the stretch of clouds.
For a moment, it seemed I could walk out of this world,
could penetrate what lived behind it,
and I knew how that turtle felt,
crawling out of the slow hatchery of sun
and rotting vegetation, inching toward the water,
on the edge of something he could not understand,
trying to be born.

NOTES:

To the Angel, Jacob kept every "dark animal among the sheep and every spotted or speckled one among the goats" for his wages.
Jacob's son, Joseph, dreamt that his brothers' "sheaves of wheat bowed to his sheaf."

The Ripped-Out Seam, "Acoma," the longest continually inhabited city in North America is an Indian pueblo built on top of a mesa.

A for Anathema, "broken tabernacle," those living on the streets, from a letter written by Mother Teresa.

Goya: Los Desastres de la Guerra, "Nada," "Nothing," Plate 69. "Agostina de Aragon," Plate 7. Last stanza, Plate 18.

The Belief in the Center of the World, only eleven people reside year round in Acoma. The city, however, is full, and open to anyone, on the feastday of San Estevan.

At the Gate of Heavenly Peace, Epcot: June, 1989, "Kuan Yin," the Chinese goddess of mercy and compassion. "Two steel balls," are Chinese exercise balls. Each one contains a metal bar that gives a distinctive sound; one sound is considered to be male, yang, the other, female, yin. They are rotated simultaneously on one hand.

Learning to Speak German, "*leibling,*" a term of endearment; "*das Wort,*" the word; "*die Welt,*" the world.

Returning Home, "kachina dolls," carved representations of kachinas, spirit messengers to the Zuñi or Hopi people. Children are given the dolls to learn the meaning of the figures and the rituals.
"It is said/ that before the kachinas were gods/ they were children drowned by the tribe," Ruth Bunzel's study on Zuñi Kachinas.

St. Rose of Lima, born Isabel de Flores, was the first native born saint of the New World. Her father imported roses to the Americas, hence, her nickname. She practiced a life of great austerity and penance.

Waiting for the Bread, the Wine, "...and what are poets for in a destitute time?" asks Hölderlin's elegy "Bread and Wine." "We hardly understand the question..." Heidigger.

"That one man,/ his lips compressed to a pure, diamond, silence, who plunges/ his way into heavy traffic," Paul Celan who drowned himself in the Seine.
"Green" was the Medieval color of hope.

Patriarchal Forest, "el aire es patriarcal y tiene alor a tristeza," "the air is patriarchal and smells of sadness." Pablo Neruda, *Los Perdidos del Bosque, The Lost Ones of the Forest*, translated by William O'Daly. Copper Canyon Press, 1986.

Trying to Find Our Way out of the Museum, "A Statue of Butter," Tibetans carve statues of butter and burn them as offerings, as prayers.

The Fear of Irrational Numbers, "an irrational number has no common standard of measurement...not expressible, etc." the quotes are a pastiche from the *Oxford English Dictionary* and *Webster's Third International Dictionary*.

The New World, "the ruins" are Anasazi, a civilization that flourished in the Southwest from the time of Christ to 1300 A.D.

Water Strider, "at this pueblo, two hostile clans," Taos Pueblo is divided into two clans, as well as physically divided, by the small stream that winds through it.

Unidentified Flowers, "hogan," the distinctive round house, made of earth with a timber framework, of traditional Navajo architecture.
Any house in which someone dies must be burnt down according to traditional Navajo beliefs.

Buddha Seesaw, Avalokiteśvara renounced Buddhahood and remained in this world out of compassion for it. Called "With a Pitying Look" by the Tibetans or "He Who Looks With the Eyes," by the Mongolians, or "Lord of the World" in Indochina, Avalokiteśvara represents mercy and compassion. The Japanese worship him as Kannon and the Chinese as the feminine Kuan Yin. The god is sometimes feminine, sometimes masculine, and has been portrayed in a variety of forms, one with a thousand arms, another with eleven heads (his head split out of grief at the number of beings yet to be saved in the world), and is the creator of this world.

Body Politic, "In this painting," *New Growth*, by Leah Kosh.

Dredging for the Face of the Earth, "angel peak," Angel Peak Monument in Mew Mexico; one of the angel's wings has eroded away. "Pedernal," a mesa, near Abiqui Lake, in view of the "red and yellow cliffs" of Ghost Ranch.
"Like the Hindhu myth of creation," in Hindhu belief, everything originated in an ocean of churning milt.

Marsyas Heard the Notes of Becoming, Marsyas, a flute-playing satyr, was flayed alive by Apollo. He challenged the god to a musical contest and won; Apollo then punished the judge and won the second contest, for which the wager was Marsyas' life.

Almost-Human, Nietzsche, *Human, All Too Human*.

The Matachines, dances that originated in medieval Spain that are still danced, though altered, in New Mexico. "*La Malinche*," the Native American woman whose linguistic skills aided Cortes in the conquest.

Cafe Without Angels, "two perched on the self-same branch," from the *Bhagavadgĩtā*. "Two birds perch on the self-same branch; one eats the fruits thereof; the other looks on in silence." "That last bird with no color, that sings softly, and travels alone," San Juan de la Cruz said the conditions of the solitary bird are five; only three are mentioned here.

Verbo Divino, the epigraph is the entire text of the poem, *Verbo Divino*, "Divine Word," by San Juan de la Cruz. "Pregnant with the divine word, the Virgin comes this way, if you will shelter her."
"Infant god and his prophet" Leonardo da Vinci's *The Virgin of the Rocks*.

Almacita Creek, "almacita," "little soul."

The quote from Osip Mandelstam's *Tristina* is from Bruce McClelland's translation. Barrytown, New York: Station Hill Press, 1987.

The epigraph for *Volte* is from *The Survivor: an anatomy of life in the death camps* by Terrence Des Pres. Oxford: Oxford, 1976.

BIOGRAPHICAL NOTE:

REBECCA SEIFERLE was born in 1951 in Boulder, Colorado. As a girl and young woman she attended 20 schools in various parts of the country. She received an "external degree" from the University of the State of New York. From 1986 – 1988 she was a member of the New Mexico Artists-in-the-Schools Program. From 1988 – 1989 she worked as a substitute teacher and librarian at the Navajo Academy, a preparatory school for gifted Navajo students. She is currently an English instructor at San Juan Community College. She is married and has two children. She makes her home in Bloomfield, New Mexico.

Poetry from The Sheep Meadow Press

Desire for White
Allen Afterman (1991)

Early Poems
Yehuda Amichai (1983)

Travels
Yehuda Amichai (1986)

Poems of Jerusalem and Love Poems
Yehuda Amichai (1992)

Father Fisheye
Peter Balakian (1979)

Sad Days of Light
Peter Balakian (1983)

Reply from Wilderness Island
Peter Balakian (1988)

5 A.M. in Beijing
Willis Barnstone (1987)

Wheat Among Bones
Mary Baron (1979)

The Secrets of the Tribe
Chana Bloch (1980)

The Past Keeps Changing
Chana Bloch (1992)

Memories of Love
Bohdan Boychuk (1989)

Brothers, I Loved You All
Hayden Carruth (1978)

Orchard Lamps
Ivan Drach (1978)

A Full Heart
Edward Field (1977)

Stars in My Eyes
Edward Field (1978)

New and Selected Poems
Edward Field (1987)

Embodiment
Arthur Gregor (1982)

Secret Citizen
Arthur Gregor (1989)

Nightwords
Samuel Hazo (1987)

Leaving the Door Open
David Ignatow (1984)

The Flaw
Yaedi Ignatow (1983)

The Ice Lizard
Judith Johnson (1992)

The Roman Quarry
David Jones (1981)

Claims
Shirley Kaufman (1984)

Summers of Vietnam
Mary Kinzie (1990)

The Wellfleet Whale
Stanley Kunitz (1983)

The Moonlit Upper Deckerina
Naomi Lazard (1977)

The Savantasse of Montparnasse
Allen Mandelbaum (1987)

Aerial View of Louisiana
Cleopatra Mathis (1979)

The Bottom Land
Cleopatra Mathis (1983)

The Center for Cold Weather
Cleopatra Mathis (1989)

To Hold in My Hand
Hilda Morley (1983)

A Quarter Turn
Debra Nystrom (1991)

Ovid in Sicily
Ovid-translated by
Allen Mandelbaum (1986)

About Love
John Montague (1993)

The Keeper of Sheep
Fernando Pessoa (1986)

Collected Poems: 1935-1992
F. T. Prince (1993)

Dress of Fire
Dahlia Ravikovitch (1978)

The Window
Dahlia Ravikovitch (1989)

Whispering to Fool the Wind
Alberto Ríos (1982)

Five Indiscretions
Alberto Ríos (1985)

The Lime Orchard Woman
Alberto Ríos (1988)

Taps for Space
Aaron Rosen (1980)

Traces
Aaron Rosen (1991)

The Nowhere Steps
Mark Rudman (1990)

Hemispheres
Grace Schulman (1984)

Every Room We Ever Slept In
Jason Shinder (1993)

Divided Light: Father and Son Poems
Edited by Jason Shinder (1983)

The Common Wages
Bruce Smith (1983)

Trilce
César Vallejo (1992)

Women Men
Paul Verlaine (1979)

The Courage of the Rainbow
Bronislava Volková (1993)

Lake
Daniel Weissbort (1993)

Poems of B.R. Whiting
B. R. Whiting (1992)

Flogging the Czar
Robert Winner (1983)

Breakers
Ellen Wittlinger (1979)

Landlady and Tenant
Helen Wolfert (1979)

Sometimes
John Yau (1979)

Flowers of Ice
Imants Ziedonis (1987)

Other Titles from The Sheep Meadow Press

Kabbalah and Consciousness
Allen Afterman (1992)

Collected Prose
Paul Celan (1986)

Dean Cuisine
Jack Greenberg and
James Vorenberg (1990)

The Notebooks of David Ignatow
David Ignatow (1984)

A Celebration for Stanley Kunitz
Edited by Stanley Moss (1986)

Interviews and Encounters with Stanley Kunitz
Edited by Stanley Moss (1993)

The Stove and Other Stories
Jakov Lind (1983)

Two Plays
Howard Moss (1980)

Arshile Gorky
Harold Rosenberg (1985)

Literature and the Visual Arts
Edited by Mark Rudman (1989)

The Stories and Recollections of Umberto Saba
Umberto Saba (1992)

The Tales of Arturo Vivante
Arturo Vivante (1990)

Will the Morning Be Any Kinder than the Night?
Irving Wexler (1991)

The Summers of James and Annie Wright
James and Annie Wright (1981)

— NOTES —